CW00858417

1

ALSO BY VAL R. BROWN

The Girl in the Velvet Slippers

A Bit of What You Fancy...

A Little Bit More ...

Freedom's
Progress

Val R. Brown

For Mary, always a friend

Acknowledgements

Sincere thanks to Rebecca for her kindness in volunteering to proof-read my book.

ISBN-13: 978-1523967353

ISBN-10: 1523967358

CONTENTS

(page numbers are relevant only to the printed version of this book)

A Mysterious Letter

Hurray! Angie stowed her carry-on bag and flopped into her comfy seat by the window. After all the frantic flurry of the past couple of weeks, she'd finally made it and could at last sit back and relax for a few hours. This was sheer luxury and she intended to savour every precious minute of it.

How had she arrived at this state of affairs when she'd seemed to be rolling along quite comfortably in her cosy little rut?

It all started on a Tuesday which, for the most part, had been quite unremarkable but underwent a rapid change when she collected her mail, as usual, from her box downstairs at the entrance to her apartment block. She'd flicked through the pile, rammed the junk mail into the trash can, retained the bills, and was left with a single, large, brown envelope which looked innocuous enough until she turned it over and spotted the U.K. stamp. That moment was the trigger to everything that happened thereafter.

Her curiosity aroused, she swiftly tore open the envelope to investigate the contents. Inside was a letter on headed notepaper from a firm of solicitors, Stephens, Hobson and Wilson, whose head office was in London. They were acting as executors of a will belonging to a deceased client who had requested that his/her identity should not be revealed at this stage of the proceedings. They had information which could prove to be to Angie's advantage but it was a condition of the will that the legatee could only be given the full details by making a personal visit to their office within six months of the date of notification. All costs for her trip would be accounted for within the monies bequeathed in the aforementioned will.

Angie made her distracted way up to her apartment, her head in a spin. Mysterious correspondence like this only happened to people in movies or, perhaps, in books. It was many years since she'd lived in the U.K. and she could think of no one who would have remembered her in their will. Most of her older relatives had long since passed away and, as far as she was aware, her brother and cousins were still hale and hearty. All contact with friends had been lost over the many years she'd spent in U.S.A. Had the solicitors misidentified her? Had something happened to her brother? Angie dismissed the latter possibility; after Tony left the Army he bought a bar in Spain where he'd settled into a happy, but far from prosperous, lifestyle. Was this a hoax of some sort?

Any further thoughts on the matter were interrupted by a cheery, "Hi Mom. It all went good today. I met up with the guys over at Chuck's this afternoon and we made progress on a whole bunch of arrangements. It sure is looking like Europe Here We Come!"

His mother looked up with a smile. "I've no doubt you'll have a fantastic time. What do you think of this?" She handed over the solicitors' letter.

Rusty quickly read the contents and gave a low, slow whistle. "Wow, Mom. This is somethin' else. Who do you know over there who would do this? What deep, dark secrets have you been keeping from me? Do you think it turns out that we're actually dim and distant relations of Lord Somebody-or-Other who has no closer heir to his estate?"

Angie laughed heartily. "I confess I'm feeling pretty dim at the moment because I can't think of anyone I know who would do this. D'you think someone's playing a practical joke on me?"

"Let's find out. Have you been in touch with them yet?"

"Give me a chance, Rusty. I've just got home. I haven't even opened the refrigerator yet."

"The refrigerator can wait. If this is genuine, we should celebrate tonight. Give them a call."

His youthful enthusiasm amused his mother. "Hold your horses, Speedy. There'll be nobody there unless some dedicated person has decided to burn the midnight oil. Don't forget the U.K. is several hours ahead of us. You'll certainly need to remember that when you do the trip because I don't want to be woken up by telephone calls in the middle of the night."

By this time Rusty was tapping away at his laptop. "I've got them Mom. They're a long- established firm and so it looks as though it's for real. You've got to go and find out what it's all about."

"Part of me would like to take the plunge but it's not as easy as it might seem. Who would look after the company?"

"Take the plunge? We're only talking about a visit to London. People do it all the time. Take the plunge? It won't even cost you a dime and as far as the company's concerned, haven't you heard about IT? If you would just give her the opportunity, Lauren could see that everything runs O.K., with you and your laptop at the end of the telephone in the unlikely event that something should go wrong. I can't remember when you last had a vacation. With me in Europe, it'll be pretty quiet around here so take the leap. Don't be boring."

"I'll think about it but I'm not celebrating until I've found out more about it. I'll telephone first thing tomorrow."

For the next twenty-four hours, thoughts of the anonymous benefactor consumed Angie's every waking moment. She contacted the solicitors, who confirmed the legitimacy of their letter, assuring her they would

11

make all arrangements for her trip if she decided to avail herself of the offer. However, despite her pleas, they could give her no further information about the legacy other than that contained in their letter of notification.

Rusty's words had hit home and hit hard, creating a sense of unease. Since he'd become more independent, spending his vacations with friends of his own age, Angie hadn't bothered to go on vacation, making the unrelenting responsibility of her job the reason for being a stay-at-home. Now she questioned whether that, perhaps, was just a convenient excuse and in reality it was all down to apathy on her part. The routine of going into the office every day to build up the business, then the need to maintain their position within the industry, had lulled her into a sense of inertia as far as her private life was concerned. Her son's words, "Don't be boring," constantly rang in her ears. Perhaps she'd already become boring and this was his way of jolting her out of it.

The more she thought about her situation the more she had to admit to herself that this letter was the most exciting thing that had happened to her in ages. Yes, perhaps she had allowed herself to become very dull, unlike the Angie of old. She was convinced she would plummet in Rusty's estimation if she didn't follow through with a trip to London and that knowledge weighed heavily on her mind, but it wasn't her only motivation. Once over her initial shock, Angie found herself warming to the idea of a little adventure. Those butterflies in the stomach hadn't fluttered for a long time and she relished their return.

Her decision made, Angie set a date for her trip, two weeks ahead, after which she threw herself wholeheartedly into re-planning her business routine. Some appointments were brought forward while others needed to be reassigned; life became one mad whirl. Fortunately, her assistant, Lauren, was happy to take over the reins in her boss's absence, with Leon, a senior manager within the company, as back-up. Daily contact would be made with Angie, a self-confessed control freak, to keep her in the loop. Everything possible had been done so that things would continue to run smoothly while she was in the U.K.

The days appeared to fly by and in what seemed like no more than the blink of an eye, Rusty and Co. had slung their heavy packs on their backs and set out for Europe. Twenty-four hours later, Angie followed them to the airport also to set out for Europe, but more specifically, London, England.

Return to the U.K.

"Good morning. This is Captain David Penhalligon. I'm your pilot today and my colleague, Tim Bennett, is… Angie was vaguely aware of the drone of the captain's voice in the background as she busied herself, settling in for the long journey ahead. First she slackened her sandals for comfort and then she rummaged amongst life's essentials in her capacious, leather handbag until she found her phone and earpiece. Next, before finally leaning back to fasten her seat belt, she removed the sick disposal bag from her airline welcome pack. Silently, but rather showily, she undid the top of the bag, blew into it and placed it conspicuously on her lap.

The passenger in the adjacent seat turned to her sympathetically. "Feeling like that already are you? Would you like me to buzz for the stewardess?"

Putting on her pathetic, 'wan' look, Angie gave him a weak smile. "No, thank you. I'll probably be quite alright; this is just precautionary. I do tend to suffer from motion sickness but I find that if I sit very quietly, listening to my music, I can cope much better and sometimes I don't even have to resort to my sick bag."

The man gave her an understanding look and, commendably, out of consideration for her condition, spoke very little to her for the entire length of the journey.

The plane was rolling forward. Sitting bolt upright, Angie gripped the armrest and braced her feet. Soon, it would be that special moment; the one that, for her, never failed to thrill. She listened intently for that magical sound; that surge of power, the thrust of the engines when they exploded into life. This was her favourite part of the flight. With ever-increasing speed, they were off, hurtling down the runway with the engines roaring, deafening, until suddenly, miraculously, they had lift-off and were soaring upwards, up into the blue like a huge, glorious bird.

Angie smiled. It was quite a while since she'd been in a plane, but the old thrill was still there. She thought back to the first time she had flown. The plane had been going in the opposite direction then, taking her to the land of her dreams, the great. U.S. of A. A lady in a smart blue costume, accompanied by a heady cloud of duty-free perfume, had taken the seat next to her.

"Are you traveling alone, dear?" she enquired.

"Yes," replied Angie. "I'm going to start a new job in New York."

"How exciting. Have you ever worked abroad before?"

"No. I've always wanted to and now it's coming true. I can't believe it."

"Tell me ...," continued the over-fragranced, over-friendly lady in a conversation which lasted for most of the journey. By the time they reached New York Angie didn't know whether the heavy perfume or the constant chatter was the problem, but what she did know, with pounding certainty, was that she had a splitting headache and couldn't get off the plane quickly enough. She'd learned her lesson well from that experience. Vowing never to repeat the horror of non-stop babble, she devised the sick bag routine which had proved to be remarkably successful at repelling small talk.

Angie set her seat to the recline position and closed her eyes, shutting out the world around her while she took a little wander down memory lane; it seemed so long ago since she'd left her old life behind her. She must have seemed unbelievably naïve, setting out to cross the ocean, all on her own, without knowing anything of the world. Born in a small Derbyshire village, which most of its inhabitants believed was the centre of the universe, she had never travelled very far and, indeed, had never even seen London until her

American job interview took her there. It seemed incredible now; the capital city and neither she nor her family had ever been there. Twenty years old and that was the first time she had struck out on her own. How times had changed.

Growing up in Millbeck hadn't been so bad. She loved its solid, grey stone buildings set in a small valley beneath the rolling green hills, all laced with a mesh of tiny streams tumbling their way down to swell the larger mill stream on its way through the village to the nearby town of Wollingford.

She'd grown up in one of those old, stone cottages. Mother and Father didn't own it. Like most of the other families in the village, they rented it from Lord Heathleigh, the biggest landowner in the area and main employer in the village. Dad was proud always to have worked for him from when he left school aged fourteen. He'd started as a general help on the estate and had gradually worked his way up to become Head Gardener. Mother had been a maid at the big house until she married Dad. Domestic service was hard work and, at the time of her marriage, she'd been delighted to become a stay-at-home housewife and mother. She never worked outside the home again but whether she remained content with the situation didn't ever come up for discussion as far as Angie could recollect. Dad always used to say that a woman's place was in the home; there was no need for women to take the jobs, which were really meant for the men, because anyone who called himself a man would provide for his wife and children. Mum rarely argued with Dad and focussed on being a thrifty housekeeper in order to eke out her husband's regular, but not very substantial, wages.

The other member of Angie's immediate family was Tony, her younger brother, born two years after her. Sometimes he was a pain in the neck when she played with her friends and he wanted to trail along with her. It was on those occasions, when Angie objected, that

Mother used to get cross and tell her she should be thankful to have a little brother. Most of the time they got along together quite well and she was always very fond of him at heart.

They'd been carefree days, those early times in Millbeck. Angie and Tony attended the village school and knew all the local children so they were never short of playmates. Although Angie got on quite well with most of them, there were two who became her special friends and for several years they were almost inseparable.

Angie's best friend was Sandra Bennett, who lived a few doors away. An only child, Sandra spent a lot of time at Angie's house where she always found a warm welcome. Her own home was usually an empty, lonely place as her mother worked long hours at a hairdressing salon in Wollingford and her father was away in the Navy. Mr. Bennett's trips home were few and far between.

The third member of their little group was Dennis Skillington, whose home was at the other end of the village. His father also worked for Lord Heathleigh; he was a car mechanic who helped maintain his Lordship's fleet of cars. Being a cheerful, sociable fellow, most of Mr. Skillington's spare time was spent in the local pub and so money was a bit scarce in their household. It was rumoured that he did a bit of poaching on the side to boost the family funds but nothing was ever proven by his accusers. Mrs. Skillington did her best to make ends meet by taking in laundry and helping with the potato picking out in the fields when the work was available. Her husband's pride didn't seem to get in the way of her going out to work but, in any case, they weren't the sort of family who worried about what the neighbours might think of them.

Dennis was generally known as Menace in and around the village. The nickname never seemed to bother him. Like his father, he was a friendly, lively character who didn't seem to worry about much. A skinny kid, with tousled, curly hair and knee socks down around his ankles, he was popular with old and young alike. A few of the boys used to tease him because he spent so much time with Angie and Sandra, but it didn't deter him. Besides, Dennis could 'look after himself' and so the other boys were wary of taking the teasing too far.

The happy trio spent much of their time roaming the hills above the village, sometimes with Tony tagging on behind them. They built dens in the bushes, paddled in the streams, caught minnows in old jam jars, joyfully revelling in their childish pursuits. Dennis seemed to know every nook and cranny of those old hills. He knew where the birds built their nests, he knew where the best bilberries grew and he knew where to find the badger setts. The girls longed to see the badgers playing so Dennis offered to take them on an evening trip if they promised to be deadly quiet as the badgers were very shy of humans. Sadly, after careful consideration they decided they'd better 'pass' on that offer because despite being given a fairly free rein in the daytime, they knew they would never be allowed out to wander the hills in the evening. Dennis thought their parents were quite unreasonable but he let the subject drop.

The seasons came and went as time marched on its relentless course until, suddenly, it was Angie's fourteenth birthday. To mark the occasion, her parents had saved hard to surprise her with the present of a shiny new bicycle. She was delighted and couldn't wait to show it to her two friends. Dennis was full of admiration.

"We'll be able to go further afield now," he exclaimed, eyes glowing and a wide grin on his freckled face. "We'll have some fun exploring new places."

Sandra, a much more reserved child said, "It's lovely Angie. You are lucky."

Turning to Dennis, Sandra asked, "What do you mean, Dennis? How can we all go exploring? In case you haven't noticed, there's only one bike amongst three people. I know I won't be having a bike for my birthday. Mother will never be able to afford it. How will you get one?"

"I already have a bike."

"You've kept that quiet, Dennis Skillington. When did you get it? What's it like. Is it an early birthday present?"

Dennis laughed. "You mean is it a first birthday present, don't you? Mother always means well but she never has enough money for presents."

"Come outside with me and I'll show you my new steed," Dennis urged them. They trooped outside into Angie's front garden. There, propped up by the front gate, was an errand boy's bicycle with a huge basket carrier on the front and "C. Packham, Grocer" emblazoned along the side. Dennis proudly waved his hand towards the bicycle. "She's a beauty isn't she?" he beamed.

The girls inspected it more closely before turning to him to ask suspiciously, "How did you get hold of this? What have you been up to now?"

"Don't you worry. It's all above board this time. George Potter is leaving school and has a job in Wollingford. He won't be delivering groceries for Mr. Packham anymore and so he gave me a nod and a wink. I went to see Mr. Packham and persuaded him that I'll be the best delivery boy he's ever had. How could he refuse when he knows it's the truth? I got the job and the use of the bike just so long as I keep it clean and in good working order. What d'you think?"

Sandra put on a brave smile. "Well, that'll be lovely for you and Angie. You can both go exploring on your bikes. You'll have to tell me all about it because I won't be able to go, not unless you give me a lift in your basket." They laughed at the thought.

The resourceful Dennis stood running his fingers through his untidy hair. "There must be something we can do, Sandra. We can't go without you. Don't worry, there's an answer to every problem; you just have to find it." He sat down on the garden wall, a thoughtful look on his face. Suddenly, he jumped up and shouted, "I've found it. I've got the answer. Dad has an old bike in the shed at the bottom of our garden. He hasn't used it in years and he won't notice, or even care, if you use it. I might have to scrounge some spare parts, here and there, but that's no big deal. I'll soon have it good as new. Well, not quite, but it will certainly get you out on the road with us."

He was as good as his word and before very long he presented the delighted Sandra with his Dad's old bike, in complete working order.

"Oh! Dennis. It's beautiful," she squealed, ringing the old bell he'd found amongst some junk. "Thank you. Thank you. Now we can all go exploring together. Let's give it a try. Where shall we go?"

Dennis was somewhat taken aback by this spontaneous show of emotion from the usually reserved Sandra. Although he was touched by her reaction, he tried to play the whole thing down. "I don't know whether I'd call it 'beautiful' Sandra, but it'll get you around. I'm glad you're pleased with it. Let's go and get Angie and hit the open road."

Twenty minutes later the little group had set out through the main street of the village, past St. Mary's Church and were heading down Vicarage Lane when Dennis exclaimed, "Oh no. It's Godly."

Angie looked in the direction of the vicarage. "It's Godfrey. He'll be back from school for the holidays. He's a bit boring, perhaps, but harmless."

20

As they drew closer, Godfrey gave a friendly wave. "Hello Angie. I was just pumping up the tyres on my new racer. What do you think of it?"

"Very smart," she replied. "We've all had new bikes too, and I'm just off on a mystery tour with Sandra and Dennis."

Godfrey, a tall, fair boy, dusted the imaginary specks of dust from his well-pressed trousers and turned his gaze towards the other two. "Hello, Sandra. "Men..., er... Dennis."

Sandra smiled sweetly. Dennis nodded his head in brief acknowledgement, muttering, "Godl...er... Godfrey. I see you're slumming it back in Millbeck again." Most of the village children attended the local school but Godfrey, as the vicar's son, was privileged to attend boarding school, paid for by a bursary from Lord Heathleigh. Even though it was an old tradition within the community, it still created an unspoken undercurrent of hostile resentment in some quarters.

"This is a change for you. I've become so accustomed to seeing you running wild, roaming the hills like a group of gypsies."

Dennis glowered, but Angie responded pleasantly, "Yes, we love the hills but now we've decided to roam the roads instead of the hills. Forward our group."

They started to remount when Godfrey, looking directly at Angie, asked, "Where are you going? Can anyone join your group?"

Dennis broke in swiftly. "Yes and no. We don't mind other people joining us, just so long as they pass the test first. Isn't that right?" he said, turning to the two girls, who, sensing an uneasy atmosphere, nodded their heads vigorously to confirm the truth in what he had said.

"So what's the test," asked Godfrey, warily.

"You have to race me up to the church gate and back on a bike."

Godfrey gave a disdainful glance at the ancient grocery bike. "Are you proposing to race me on that old boneshaker?" He laughed loudly. "It looks as though it couldn't make it to the church gate without falling apart, especially if you try to hurry it along. My bike will beat yours hands down. It's an absolute cert." He flashed a quick, furtive glance to see what effect it was having on the girls, as he stood, one hand in his pocket, his head tilted back and an arrogant smile on his thin lips.

An unsmiling Dennis replied bluntly, "It's not about the bikes; it's about the riders. You didn't wait till I'd finished telling you about the rules. We have to ride barefoot."

Disbelief spread over the elegant Godfrey's face. "Barefooted? Do you really expect me to ride barefooted? That might suit a heathen like you but I'm not accustomed to going around the village barefooted."

Sandra, who usually wouldn't say "boo" to a goose, decided to support her friend, remembering the efforts he'd made to find her a bicycle. "Come on Godfrey. Don't be boring. It's just a bit of fun. Take your shoes off."

The incorrigible Dennis grinned. "I bet he's got a hole in his sock. You're amongst friends God...Godfrey." The girls tried not to giggle, but without much success.

Pink-faced, Godfrey glanced at the sharp metal teeth on the pedals of his racer, then, making a show of looking at his expensive wristwatch, he said in a surprised tone, "Oh! Is that the time already? I can't hang around here with you and your puerile chatter. I must rush. I'd promised to play tennis, you know, the grown-up game, with Nick and his chums at the big house." Nick was Lord Heathleigh's son, the same age as Godfrey, who also attended boarding school. Turning an icy glare on Dennis, Godfrey sneered, "I hope you have a repair kit in that large basket of yours." He gave

Angie an ingratiating smile. "I'll see you at church on Sunday, Angie. Remember me to your parents."

The band of three mounted and cycled off into the distance, with Dennis making clucking noises and flapping his elbows like a chicken. Further down the road, Angie asked, "So what was that all about Dennis? I've never known you behave like that with anyone? What's Godfrey done to get you so rattled?"

"I'm sorry if I upset either of you but I just can't help myself when I'm within earshot of that patronising so-and-so. Why don't those posh schools he and Nick go to teach them to speak properly instead of sounding as though they have a plum in their mouth's? They'd get more respect round here if they spoke right. On top of that, he's just so smug with his snooty nose so far up in the air that he's going to trip over one of these days. He always needles away and although I try hard to ignore the jumped-up bore, he always manages to get my hackles up. Anyway, we don't need another member of our cycling club, do we?" Laughing and chatting easily together, they continued on their merry way.

A week later, Dennis cycled round to meet the girls at Angie's house. "I've had a rethink about not having an extra member of our cycling group."

Angie and Sandra looked at him in alarm. "You haven't apologised to that odious Godfrey and invited him to join us?" gasped Sandra.

Grinning, in his ear-to-ear style, Dennis replied, "How could I apologise? I'm not sorry." He leaned into the carrier on the front of his bike. "This is our new member," he told them, holding aloft a small black puppy. "He'll be less trouble than Godly."

The girls immediately fell in love with the little, black, furry bundle. "What sort of dog is he? Will he grow too big for your basket?" they asked.

"I'm not sure what sort of dog he is. Our dog, Lady, got out of the house when she shouldn't have and this is the result. We don't know who his father is. This little chap is the runt of the litter. Do you think we should call him Tiny?"

Together, they carefully trolled through a long list of names and finally decided on Samson, in the hope that he would grow to be healthy and strong. He became a faithful, enthusiastic member of the group.

Changes Afoot

The carefree lifestyle of the three friends continued, almost without any major change, until they were nearing the end of their last year at Wollingford High School, the year in which they reached their sixteenth birthdays. It was around that time, on a Saturday afternoon, that Mrs. Caswell, Angie's mother, heard an excited bark at the front door. "I'll get it," she called, hurrying through from the kitchen, wiping her hands on her apron. As she threw open the front door, a bundle of black fur scampered past her to sit in the kitchen doorway with an expectant look on its face. "Come in Dennis. Oh! My goodness! You've been in the wars, haven't you, or was it the usual wardrobe door that jumped out and attacked you?"

"It was something like that Mrs. Caswell. Is Angie in?"

"She's in the living room. Go through and I'll get you a cup of tea and some scones I've just taken fresh out of the oven. Come on Samson, let's see what treat I have for you today."

Angie looked up as Dennis entered the cosy living room. "What's happened Dennis? That's some shiner and you're walking with a limp. Don't try to fob me off with your usual old rubbish about walking into something. That's the third time you've had a black eye in the past few months. What's going on? Truth this time."

Dennis winced as he sat down in the comfy chair opposite the earnest Angie.

"It's so embarrassing. I wasn't going to say anything but I suppose the village tongues must be wagging anyway so I might as well tell you the real truth behind it all. Dad hasn't been himself just lately. He's always bad tempered, which isn't really him, and he's spending more time and money at the pub. Also, he's developing a bad limp but flies off the handle if anyone mentions it. When he eventually gets home from the pub, we hardly dare say a word because he goes crazy and becomes violent."

"Is that what happened last night?" asked Angie.

Dennis tried to nod his head but was in obvious discomfort.

"Mother took his dinner out of the oven and put it in front of him on the table. The rest of us had eaten at the usual time and she'd tried to keep his food warm for him, so that he wouldn't complain about her not having a meal ready for him. She'd done her best but, of course, the food had started to dry out after four hours. Dad took one look at it and with a sweep of his arm, cleared everything off the table onto the floor, cursing Mother for being so useless.

It wasn't the first time he'd done this and Mother had learned that it was best to stay silent. So, when she knelt on the floor and started to pick up the pieces, I took my cue from her, saying nothing as I knelt down beside her to help. That was all it took to set him off. He pushed me off balance, grabbed Mother and started shouting obscenities at her, accusing her of turning me and the others against him. As he raised his arm to strike her, I just managed to get to my feet to shield her. It was my turn then. He grabbed the poker and caught me around the shoulders and on the thigh. He was just going to try to get me again when the poker dropped from his grip, his face contorted into a strange kind of look and then he dropped to his knees clutching his chest. 'See what you've done,' he hissed between clenched teeth. I knew something serious was wrong with him and so, quick as a flash, I rushed over to Mrs. Hill at Fairview Cottage; being a nurse, she has a phone. When I told her what had happened, she rang for an ambulance then ran back to our place to see what she could do to help."

"Is your father all right? What happened next?"

"The ambulance from Wollingford Hospital came fairly swiftly. They wanted to take me with them to see if I had any broken bones but I told them I'd survive. I stayed at home with the little ones while Mrs. Hill went to the hospital with Mother and Father. After all she's been through just lately, with the violence as well as trying to manage on a shoestring, Mother was in a bit of a state and I was thankful Mrs. Hill was there.

It turns out that Dad had a stroke last night because he has uncontrolled sugar diabetes. He must have been feeling unwell for some time but was too stubborn to see a doctor. He likes to think of himself as the big, strong man who never ails anything. Anyway, when they examined him at the hospital they soon found out why he'd developed a limp. His right leg was black up to the knee and gangrene had set in; they don't think they'll be able to save it."

"That's terrible Dennis," gasped Angie, her big blue eyes open wide. "I feel very sorry for your dad but he's certainly put the rest of the family through the mill. If only he hadn't been so stubborn."

"Yes, I know. I think he was frightened to find out the truth about his leg but if he'd just gone to see a doctor earlier, they might have been able to save it."

"How's your mother taking it all?"

"I think she's in shock. Also, she's worrying about the money if Dad is going to be off work for a while. His job doesn't come with sick pay. I haven't dared mention it to her, but, of course, there's always the possibility that he might not be able to go back to his job. We'll be in a right pickle then."

Their conversation was interrupted by Mrs. Caswell coming through the door, carrying a big tray of tea, scones and home-made jam. "You look like you've got all the worries of the world on your shoulders today,

Dennis," she said quietly. "A nice cup of tea and a bite to eat always helps a bit. Tuck in lad. By the way, we've found ourselves with a glut of vegetables in the garden this year and there's only the four of us to eat them. I've put a few in a bag for your mother. I hope she won't be offended." A ring on the doorbell took her out to the hall again. "I'll bet that's Sandra." She was right.

It didn't take Sandra long to realize something was amiss and so Angie and Dennis, between them, quickly brought her up to date. "Have you been round to see Lord Heathleigh yet?" she asked. "He might have some part-time work for you to help out a bit until the doctors can give you a better idea about your dad's future. It must be tough being the eldest but your mother's going to need something more than what you get from your grocery round."

Sandra continued. "I have to say, Dennis, from what you've told me, it's not sounding good. If they've already said that they can't save his leg, then it's pointless hanging on to false hope. Your Dad may eventually be able to go back to work at the estate but how can he do his present job when it's so physically demanding? He might have to take on lighter duties. It's going to take some time to get him sorted out and meanwhile, you all have to survive. You can't live on fresh air."

Dennis smiled at his friend. "Don't hold back Sandra, will you."

Offering him the plate of scones, Sandra replied, "You wouldn't want me to try to hide the truth, would you? That's not the way we work but if I can help you in any way, you know I'm here for you."

"Thanks Sandra. I know that. Actually, I've been round to the Estate Office this morning to let them know about Dad. I'd already sent them a letter of application for a job when I leave school, saying I want to work outdoors and asking if they might find something suitable for me. They told me they'll find me some part-time work for the time being and will consider my job application. They warned me that they may not be able to offer me the type of work I've requested but they'll probably be able to offer me something, depending on exam. results etc. Now, what have you been up to today? I could see you had something to tell us by the way you bounced through the door."

"I've got a job; well, I've sort of got a job. I'm so excited."

"Where?" asked Angie. "Everyone's starting work except me."

"It's at a hair salon in Wollingford. Mum knows the owner. I can work as their Saturday girl until I leave school and, if I do well, they'll take me on as an apprentice hairdresser. I'll have one day off a week to go to college so that I can study to get my qualifications. It's so exciting. I'll be able to earn my own money and Mum won't have to keep worrying about whether we can afford things."

"Do you want to be a hairdresser?" asked Dennis. "You'll be indoors six days a week, breathing in those horrible scenty smells, telling people their new hairdo makes them look the image of Audrey Hepburn or Sophia Loren when really they look like the back of a bus. I can't imagine anything worse but if it's what suits you, then well done and the best of luck."

Sandra laughed gaily. "Watch out Dennis Skillington. If I need someone to practise on, I might have a go at your mop."

"Well done both of you," said Angie. "It sounds like you've got yourselves sorted. I'm still not sure what to do. Mother and Father want me to enrol at the secretarial college in Wollingford because they believe being a secretary is a good job for a woman. Also, there's always jobs for secretaries advertised in Situations Vacant. Father thinks I should get my toe in the door at The Hall and then I'd be set for life, or at least until I get married and have children. He says he'll make enquiries at the Estate Office."

Dennis looked at her. "But...?" he enquired.

"Well. It all sounds pretty boring doesn't it? Also," and she tried to blink away the tears that had welled up in her eyes, "I feel sad because everything is going to be different from now on. We've always been together on Saturdays but you'll both be working, so when will we see each other? Will we still go on bike rides? I doubt it, somehow."

Sandra put her arm around her friend's shoulders. "Yes, things will be different Angie, especially for poor Dennis here who'll just have to soldier on and see how things work out. Saturdays are going to be difficult, but we have evenings. There's several places in Wollingford where we could meet for a coffee or something, or, you could both come to our house and play the records I'm going to buy on the record player I'm planning to buy. Cheer up. It's just a change; it's not the end of the world."

Into the World of Work

A few weeks later, decisions had been made and Angie started out on her new lifestyle. After considering the options open to her, such as shop assistant, waitress, receptionist, trainee nurse, she decided she may as well please her parents by enrolling on the secretarial course at the Riverside Technical College. It was a one-year, full-time course and at the end of it she would receive certificates stating she was proficient in shorthand, typing, book-keeping and French. She'd also made arrangements to work a few hours a week in the estate office so that not only would she have some pocket money of her own but would also have a better opportunity of getting full-time work there after she had left college.

To her surprise, she quite enjoyed college initially. All the students were girls, none of whom had studied commercial subjects before and they all seemed to mix quite well. Sometimes a few of them would go out together to the cinema or to a local café.

. One group invited Angie to go dancing with them but she declined; dancing just wasn't her thing. As the year progressed, several of the girls acquired boyfriends and so there wasn't quite so much group social activity. Conversation seemed to focus more and more on boyfriends, what to wear on a date, make-up, hairstyles and how to conceal inconvenient pimples. Angie was fast becoming bored with the situation with an overwhelming feeling of being a square peg in a round hole.

Work in the Estate Office could hardly be called stimulating. Photocopying, stapling and filing bits of paper were not Angie's idea of 'inspiring'. Her occasional sessions with Sandra and Dennis at Giuseppe's Café were a beacon in her otherwise drab existence. Weekends were particularly tedious.

One Saturday afternoon, she was in her usual fireside seat, staring into space when Mrs. Caswell bustled into the room. "Penny for them?" she asked of her daughter.

"Haven't got any," returned Angie. "I'm just so bored."

"A young girl like you can't be bored; you're just being boring.   There's loads of things you could be doing instead of sitting here with a long face."

"Such as?"

"You're just not trying Angie. You could sort out some of your things for the jumble sale."

"I've passed them all on to Dennis for his young sisters."

"I'm sure you could find something, but never mind. You could ring Sandra and get your hair done; it's a bit of a mess. Ask her for a new style to perk you up."

"Hair is boring."

Not to be put off, Mrs. Caswell continued. "You could put that box of flowers on your bicycle rack and take it round to the church for Mrs. Wilson to do the arrangements for tomorrow. That would be really useful Angie; it would save your father's old legs. You might even feel like a little bicycle ride afterwards. I'd honestly be glad of your help."

The idea of doing something useful to help her parents had some appeal for Angie and so she roused herself and set out for the church. Just as she was propping up her bike on the church porch, the big oak door creaked and out came Godfrey. His usually sulky face lit up when he saw Angie minus the rest of her group.

"Hello Angie. I didn't expect to see you here on a Saturday. Why aren't you out with your friends exploring the highways and byways? Has the grocery bike finally fallen to pieces?"

"Oh, the others work on Saturdays now and so things have changed slightly. I haven't seen you for ages Godfrey. Where have you been hiding yourself? You don't seem to come home much nowadays."

"I usually spend the holidays with friends, especially Nick. You know, don't you, he lives in France with his mother most of the time, ever since his parents decided to split up. There's not much in Millbeck to interest me these days. I'm home this week to visit the parents, of course, but also because it's Nick's eighteenth birthday and his father wanted to give him a special bash in the family home. It's going to be quite an event."

"Sounds exciting."

"They've booked several groups to perform indoors and out during the evening. There's the Swinging Squirrels, Jan and the Jangles, the Rockadores and so the list goes on. The old place will certainly be swinging."

Angie was impressed. "The Rockadores were top of the charts for three weeks in a row last month. Fancy them being right here in little old Millbeck."

"I say, Angie, would you like to come? It's by invitation only, of course, but mine is for Mr. Godfrey Hoddlestone and guest. Please say you'll be my partner."

These were top groups; the invitation was very tempting. When would she get another opportunity to see them?

"When is this party? The music should be really groovy."

"It's on Nick's actual birthday, this coming Friday. Father allows me to borrow the car occasionally, now that I've passed my test. Leave your bike at home and I'll pick you up from your place at 7 o'clock."

Angie laughed; as though she would go on her bike. Godfrey cracking a joke was certainly a first. "Thank you Godfrey. That will be lovely."

"Super," he said, holding open the church door for her to deliver her box of flowers.

Angie rushed down the aisle to where a group of ladies were busy cleaning the brasses. "Hello ladies. Lovely day for it, isn't it?. Father sent these for you. Must dash."

Back home, she entered the house like a whirlwind. "Mother, do you know what time Jan's salon closes? I need an appointment for next week. Also, I need a new party dress. Something really special. I'm catching the next bus into Wollingford. D'you want to come with me?"

"Good gracious, Angie. Whatever's brought this on? One minute you're like a wilting wallflower and the next, you're rushing around like a maniac. You've got a couple of dresses you've hardly worn. Won't they do?"

"No. Godfrey's invited me to Nick's eighteenth at the big house and everyone will be dressed in the latest. I don't want to look like the country yokel. I've never been to an event like this before and I have to look the part. The Rockadores are performing."

"The Rocka...who? Who are they when they're out?"

"Oh! Mother! Don't be so square. Haven't you heard them on the wireless? Sandra is mad about them; she has all their records."

The Party

Angie floated through the living room door in a cloud of perfume. "What do you think?" she asked her parents. "Will I do?" Wearing her new silk shift dress in a delicate shade of lemon, with a white trim, she twirled as she spoke, then looked at her parents expectantly.

"You'll knock'em for six," her father said proudly. "You'll be the belle of the ball. It's certainly going to be a grand do up yonder tonight. We've got the garden looking its best and the fellows have spent all afternoon hanging lights in the trees. Just tell that young Godfrey Hoddlestone to drive carefully and make sure he gets you home on time."

"He'll look after her alright," chided Mrs. Caswell. "He's a vicar's son."

"Since when did that make any difference?" was the cynical reply.

Unabashed, his wife continued. "They'll make a lovely pair. You never know what might come of this."

Angie looked at her mother sharply. "Don't start getting any romantic notions Mother. I've no intentions of being a pair with Godfrey Hoddlestone or anyone else for that matter. I'm simply going with him tonight because I've never been to this kind of do before and I'd like to see what it's like. There he is now. Don't wait up. I'll be alright. Bye." She grabbed her little evening bag and was gone.

Godfrey was looking very suave in his dark suit and white shirt. In true gentlemanly fashion, he came round to open the door for Angie; feeling almost regal, she sank back in her seat, looking forward to having the time of her life.

Back in the driving seat Godfrey enquired, "Straight to the party or would you like to go for a spin first? It's a lovely evening for a drive."

"I don't want to miss a moment of Nick's birthday party, Godfrey. Let's go straight there." Seeing the disappointed look on his face, she added, "Perhaps we can go for a drive another time."

A few minutes later they turned into the tree-lined drive to Holliwell Hall. They could hear the strains of the music as they drew nearer, until, finally, a fairyland of colour, lights and gaiety opened up before their astonished gaze. The dignified, old stone house, usually so quietly restrained, now looked out on a throng of colourful, youthful, noisy guests.

They eventually found Nick near the champagne fountain, chatting to a couple of friends. Godfrey strode up to shake him by the hand, saying exuberantly, "Happy birthday, old boy. Your old man's turned up trumps tonight." He acknowledged the two young men. "Charles." "Julian." Putting his arm around Angie to usher her forward a little, he continued, "You remember Angie, don't you?" Nick was obviously struggling until Godfrey added, "Angie, Angie Caswell. We all used to play together in the early days. Her father still works here."

Nick's face lit up. "Of course I remember Angie. I'd recognize those blonde curls anywhere. You're all grown-up! I'm delighted to see you again after so long. Waiter, champagne for the lady." His speech was slightly slurred and he staggered a little as he turned to speak to his friends in French, telling them, "This is Angie, the gardener's daughter. We used to play together in the woods and gardens."

Charles, who also looked slightly the worse for drink, raised an eyebrow suggestively, responding in French, saying, "Really? It sounds like the Lady Chatterley relationship in reverse." He looked immensely pleased with himself. Julian, also speaking in French, added, "I wouldn't mind a frolic in the woods with this little nymph. Has she brought any friends?" All three laughed raucously while Godfrey, whose French was probably a bit shaky, looked somewhat embarrassed and raised a slight smile.

This kind of talk was the last thing Angie had expected from her old friend. She felt sick in the pit of her stomach but she was determined to keep her cool. Smiling sweetly, she turned to Nick. Speaking in fluent French, she said to him, "I've been so looking forward to meeting the grown-up Nick to see if you've changed at all. However, I see you haven't changed one jot; still the lavatory humour and the crass, juvenile behaviour. I suppose your reports are still saying 'room for improvement'." Nick's jaw dropped.

"As for your friends," she continued, still in perfect French, her eye fixed intently on the dapper visitors, "may I ask where you come from?" Looking quite shocked, Charles stammered, "Henley-on-Thames."

"Ah!" she replied "I knew by your dreadful accent that you couldn't possibly be French. I suggest that when you return to Henley-on-Thames, you ask them to teach you a few manners, as well as improving your French. You see, you may be surprised to learn that our state schools around here teach languages to a very high standard. Also, we learn good manners from the cradle and your extremely rude behaviour towards me this evening is not socially acceptable."

The three young men looked stunned, realizing she'd understood every word they'd uttered. Without giving them a chance to reply, Angie put down her untouched glass of champagne, saying, in English, "Please excuse us. Godfrey and I are going down to the front lawn to listen to the music. Enjoy the party boys."

The music turned out to be every bit as good as she'd expected and Godfrey, too, seemed to be having a good

37

time. They joined in with the enthusiastic crowd, clapping, cheering and dancing disco-style. Any thoughts of Nick and his rude companions were temporarily erased from Angie's mind.

"Let's go and have a drink," she suggested after a particularly energetic number. We can always come back to hear the rest."

"O.K.," said Godfrey, "but first I want to show you something. I don't think you'll have seen it before; it's a fairly recent installation."

They strolled across the lawn, in an easterly direction, towards a copse of trees, leaving the music and lights behind. Reaching the edge of the small wood, Godfrey stopped. "What d'you think of this? Lord Heathleigh commissioned it from a chap who makes naturalistic-shaped furniture from local wood. This bench came from a tree on the estate." He took out his snowy white handkerchief to flick off any stray leaves or seeds, saying to Angie, "Let's just sit in the peace for a few minutes. Look, it's a full moon tonight. It's so beautiful, just like you." Angie, sitting beside him on the bench, gave a small, embarrassed laugh. Wrapping one of her curls around his finger, Godfrey continued. "I've always loved your hair Angie. No one has blonde curls quite like yours. You look gorgeous tonight." He leaned towards her. "Mmmm, your hair smells like a summer garden; I could lose myself in that." Angie squirmed, feeling somewhat uncomfortable with the unexpected turn of events; little did she know that the evening had even more surprises in store for her. Breathing heavily, Godfrey swiftly slipped his arm down around her shoulders, kissing her on the face and then fully on the lips. Angie tried to move but found herself completely trapped in his vice-like grip. Next, she felt his other sweaty hand caressing her knee then slowly start to slither underneath the hemline of her dress. She mustered all her strength and screeched at him, "No, no. GET OFF!"

As she struggled frantically, she was vaguely aware of the bark of a dog coming from the direction of the wood. Next moment, a snarling, growling creature was snapping at Godfrey's legs. His own safety overcoming his passion, Godfrey immediately released his hold on Angie to try to beat off his vicious canine attacker. Amidst the confusion of growling and screaming, she heard the sound of heavy footsteps pounding the ground behind her, then a voice in her ear commanded, "Run, Angie. Run." Without another thought, she took to her heels and ran like the wind, never stopping until she reached the main gates.

Home was not very far to go but it was certainly a lonely, wretched walk back for Angie on that occasion. She'd started the evening full of excitement and anticipation, never expecting to be insulted by Nick and his friends or to be subjected to Godfrey's low behaviour. She felt so degraded. Why did any of them think they had the right to treat her in that way? Was it just her or did they behave like that towards all girls? Initially, she felt very sorry for the dishevelled, sobbing person she'd become, walking home all on her own from what was supposed to be the most glamorous evening of her life. However, it didn't take long for that self-pity to turn to anger. Who did they think they were? What made them think they could be so patronising towards her? Why did Godfrey believe it was O.K. to behave in that way towards her? She'd never allow herself to be treated like that again. She'd show them.

She opened the door quietly and crept silently up the stairs to the safety of her own little bedroom.

The Aftermath

Next morning, Mrs. Caswell wanted to hear all about the party. Did Angie enjoy it? Did she see Nick? Did she meet some nice people? What did they wear?

A weary Angie tried to fend off the inquisition. "Yes I met Nick and he hasn't changed at all. He's ruder than ever. I can't remember what people were wearing. The music was good but I came home early because I had a headache and because I found the whole thing very boring, as are your questions mother."

Undeterred, Mrs. Caswell started off again with, "Whatever did Godfrey think about you wanting to leave early?" She never received an answer because her husband broke into the conversation. "Leave off, Marjorie. Can't you take a hint? The lass doesn't want to talk about it. Now, I thought you were going to the shops. Don't forget my tobacco."

Peace reigned in the little stone house until Mrs. Caswell burst in with her shopping, dying to relate the latest gossip. "I bumped into Doris Cartwright in the baker's. You know, she does a bit of cleaning at the vicarage. Well, she told me they had to call an ambulance up to the big house last night. It was for Godfrey." She paused for breath, looking to see what effect her news had on her two listeners.

"Apparently, a stray dog had appeared out of nowhere and attacked him. He was having a breath of fresh air over by that little wood at the time. He tried to escape by running away but ran into a tree in the dark. He has two black eyes and a broken nose, as well as bites and scratches on his legs. He was rushed off to hospital in an ambulance but he's back home now. Doris says he looks in a bad way."

"Did they catch the dog?" asked Mr. Caswell. "It might attack again."

Angie remained silent, casually flicking through a magazine on her lap.

"She didn't say whether or not they had the dog. Will you be going round to see poor Godfrey, Angie? It must have happened after he brought you home."

"He didn't bring me home and no, I won't be going to see him. Now, mother, do you mind if we drop the subject?"

"I don't know what gets into you sometimes, our Angie. I just thought you'd like to know as Godfrey's your friend."

Mr. Caswell looked up from filling his pipe. "If you're going in the direction of the kitchen Mother, I wouldn't mind a cup of tea to go with this smoke." His wife finally took the hint.

Left alone with his daughter Ted Caswell remarked quietly, "I don't know what went on last night Angie and I'm not going to ask, but something's wrong. Are you alright?"

"Thanks Dad. I just want to forget the whole thing but don't worry, I'm alright. I've been thinking though, would you be upset if I handed in my notice at the estate office? I fancy a change and thought I might look for another part-time job."

"I don't mind as long as you leave on good terms. Always make sure you can go back to a place because you never know what the future might bring. If a change is what you're after, then have a change, although you needn't work at all until after you've finished at college."

"I know that Dad, but I like to feel I'm earning my own pocket money. There's a part-time job going in Wollingford that I have my eye on. I might go to see what that's all about."

A comfortable silence settled on the room as her father puffed contentedly on his pipe and read his newspaper.

Later that day Dennis called round with Samson in tow. Angie was on her own. The dog settled himself at her feet, licking her hand as she petted him.

Dennis took a small package out of his pocket. "I thought you might like this," he said, grinning a little sheepishly as he passed it over to his friend. "You left it behind when you did your Cinderella act."

A curious Angie opened the wrapping to reveal her evening bag; she smiled for the first time that day. "I thought it might be you. I've never really thought of you as a knight in shining armour, but I can't tell you how glad I was when you appeared last night and I was thankful you were with him too," she said, caressing Samson's curly black coat. "I didn't know you could be so fierce."

"How come you were there Dennis? I didn't see you at the party but as soon as I heard the bark, I knew it was Samson."

"I often take Samson for a walk in those woods at night. Your dad knows and has asked me to keep an eye out for poachers." They both laughed heartily, knowing that his own father was the most notorious poacher in Millbeck. "I didn't realize you'd be at the party with the posh people but as soon as Samson heard your raised voice, he was off. I just followed him. I never liked that Godfrey Hoddlestone and when I spotted what was going on, I just saw red. I called him every low name I could think of, then when he gave me a smart-ass reply about you, that was it. I thumped him good and proper and I feel no remorse. He had it coming. I told him to watch his step or I'd do it again, then I called Samson off and we disappeared back into the wood."

"Mother told me the story on the village grapevine is that Godfrey ran into a tree while trying to get away from a savage stray dog. He was eventually carted off to hospital in an ambulance and this morning he's nursing two shiners and a broken nose."

The unrepentant Dennis grinned mischievously. "As you know, heathen that I am, I never go to church, but it might be worth a visit this Sunday just to see Godly suffering for his sins."

The Coliseum

The job Angie had seen advertised was for a part-time usherette at the Coliseum, the cinema on the main street in Wollingford. It was a small, local theatre, privately-owned by a Mr. and Mrs. Roper. Angie arranged an interview for the following Tuesday, after she'd finished her day at college.

Mrs. Roper, known to all and sundry as Madge, was on her usual stool in the box office when Angie arrived. She was a pleasant, motherly soul. "Oh! You're the one who's applied for the job. I know your face but you're not from Wollingford are you? Don't you come from Millbeck way? Isn't that your father, the gardener at Holiwell Hall? I often see him coming into town in the estate van." Madge knew everything about everyone. "Tony's just setting up for the next performance. I'll get him for you before it begins."

"Janet, have you got a minute? Will you go and tell Tony someone's here about the usherette job?" A girl, a little older than Angie, wearing an usherette's uniform, disappeared through a swing door. Minutes later, Mr. Roper appeared in the foyer and beckoned Angie over to sit beside him on one of the plush crimson sofas. He was a middle-aged man, of medium height, smartly dressed in a grey suit, pin-striped shirt and florid tie adorned with a jewelled tie pin. His dark hair was parted down one side and sleeked back with hair cream; he reeked of cheap aftershave. He offered Angie a limp, slightly moist handshake.

"Nice to meet you Angie. I'm Anthony Roper, the owner and manager of The Coliseum."

"Co-owner," came a voice from the box office.

Unperturbed, he continued. "We're a friendly bunch here and so everyone calls me Tony." He smiled widely, revealing the yellow teeth of a heavy smoker. "We're a small team. You've met my wife, Madge, then there's Janet, the usherette, George the general help and Connie, the cleaner. We're a happy crew, getting along together very well. I'm sure you'll fit in well. Your duties would include showing customers to their seats and selling ice creams in the intervals. You'll certainly look very smart in the uniform we provide and be a very popular ice cream girl." He gave a quick glance towards his wife. "We pay the going rate and what we ask from you in return is absolute reliability. We have to know that you will turn up for your shift as we carry no surplus staff."

Angie was very excited about the job, especially as Mr. Roper had said that the usherettes could stand at the back of the cinema during performances, so she'd be able see all the latest films free of charge. She was not too sure about Mr. Roper. It felt odd to call a man by his first name when he was so much older than herself; he came across as what her mother would describe as "greasy." However, Madge was nice and the job sounded like fun. Angie accepted and took on her new role of cinema usherette.

Everything got off to a flying start and Angie thought she was going to enjoy her new job. The rest of the staff were friendly, all getting on with their own work and the whole place seemed to run like clockwork. She'd been there about a week when Anthony Roper walked past, at the beginning of her shift.

"Have you ever seen inside a projection room?" he asked. "That's where it all happens; it's extremely interesting."

"To be honest, it's not something I've ever thought about," replied Angie.

"I know you'll find it interesting," persisted Tony. "When you've shown everyone to their seats, come up and I'll show you around."

Angie felt it would be rude to refuse when he was being kind, so she made her way up the stairs and knocked on the door of the projection room. Tony opened the door and beckoned her inside a tiny, dimly lit room that emanated the familiar stench of cheap toiletries.

"There's not much space in here," he laughed, "and yet this room is the very heart beat of the cinema." He locked the door behind her.

"Why do you need the door locked, Tony?" she enquired, frowning.

"Like I say, this is a very important place and I can't have just anyone barging in here. Now let me show you. We're a bit old-fashioned in the way of equipment, but it runs as smoothly as ever. Look at this beauty." He patted a big, gleaming, brass panel on the wall by the door displaying four large switches. "These are the master switches; they govern everything. How about this panel for good old-fashioned craftsmanship?"

"Very nice," murmured Angie, completely underwhelmed and unable to join in his enthusiasm for brass backing-plates.

Tony put his arm lightly on Angie's shoulder and turned her towards the table in the centre of the cramped room. "It's a bit of a squeeze in here, I know, but if you'd just like to slip into this chair, I'll explain how the projection system works." Angie could hear the equipment whirring and decided it might actually be quite interesting to learn how the picture was projected onto the screen, so she relaxed and prepared herself to listen and learn.

While Angie occupied the only available chair in the room, Tony stood behind her. As she listened, she became conscious of his left hand on her left shoulder; he used his right hand to point to the various bits of equipment and their switches. She tried to focus on what he was telling her but was all too aware that his left hand was gradually slithering down, under her armpit and was slowly making its way towards her breast.

"I think that's enough Tony," she said. "It's time I went back downstairs."

Tony cupped her right breast with his other hand. "You know you like it. You're a proper tease, aren't you? You young ones are all the same."

Angie couldn't move; she was trapped tightly between the table and the chair, with the weight of Tony Roper on her shoulders. "Get off, you pervert," she shouted, "I'll tell your wife", but undeterred, he started to kiss the top of her head, keeping his hands in place. Angie had to think quickly; there'd be no Samson to save her this time, it was all down to her. In desperation, she made a super-human effort to stretch an arm out towards the switches on the table and flicked them at random; that did the trick.

"You little bitch," he roared, releasing his hold on her and leaning forward, trying to pull her hands off his precious switches. Having diverted his attention, quick as a flash, Angie flicked her head backwards and caught him on his nose. His reflex reaction was to put his hands up to his face and that's when Angie seized her opportunity to make a dash towards the door. She paused briefly by the treasured brass plate and enjoyed the satisfaction of rapidly flicking every single switch. As she turned the key in the door to make her escape, she could hear the equipment in the projection room spluttering to a halt. Tony's furious oaths and obscenities floated on the air behind her as she fled down the stairs and into the safety of the ladies toilets. Alone in there, she caught her breath and then sobbed and sobbed for what seemed like ages but in reality, was only a few moments. Catching sight of herself in the big, gilt-framed mirror, she dabbed her swollen, red eyes with cold water. She tidied her hair and straightened her clothes while telling her reflection, "I don't know how I'll do it, but I'll certainly show you Mr. Anthony Roper."

As she walked through the foyer, she could hear slow hand clapping and the stamping of feet in the auditorium. Ignoring it, she made her way to the rear door of Madge's box office.

"I'm handing in my notice Madge, effective from today."

Madge swivelled round on her stool to address her. "What's brought this on? Are you alright? You don't look your usual self."

Angie said quietly, "I'm all right thanks, Madge. As I said, I'm leaving and I don't want to discuss it."

Madge gave her a knowing look. "I wondered where you'd got to; he's been showing you his projection equipment hasn't he?" Angie nodded.

"I should have known better," said Madge. "I should have warned you but he promised he wouldn't do it again. That man's made me so many promises, but they're all like pie crusts, made to be broken."

"I'm sorry Madge," said Angie. "I never did anything to encourage him. He's so much older than me. I never dreamt anything like this would happen."

"It's not your fault, love," soothed Madge. "It's that deluded husband of mine. He's always had wandering hands. Age doesn't come into it with him; he thinks he's God's gift to women in general. I'll have his guts for garters this time."

By then, the big double exit doors from the cinema had been thrown open and an angry audience was flooding into the foyer. Many of them were knocking on the front window of the box office, demanding their money back for a show that they hadn't seen in full.

Angie slipped away, leaving Madge to deal with the problem. Her mind was occupied with how she would show that Tony Roper that he'd made a big mistake when he tangled with Angie Caswell.

That evening she met Sandra and Dennis in their usual café and lost no time in bringing them up to scratch with everything that had happened at the Coliseum.

"Ugh! Dirty old man," was Sandra's reaction.

"Well, I feel like landing him one," said Dennis, then, with his irrepressible grin, "but it sounds like you've done enough damage to him already. I think he'll cross the road, terrified, the next time he sees you."

"I'm not finished with him yet," said Angie grimly. "I've got a plan; are you going to help me out?" By the time she'd outlined what she intended to do, the three were rolling with laughter.

They stayed at Giuseppe's slightly later that evening. Once it was dark, they made their way to the car park on the side of the cinema, to the reserved parking spot in the corner where the car park ran alongside the main street. The impressive black notice on the cinema wall read, "Reserved for Mr. A. Roper." The car park was empty on that particular evening as performances had been suspended until further notice, due to unforeseen circumstances.

Angie had come prepared, "Stop giggling you two and keep an eye out." She took from her bag two tiny pots of modelling paint, one black and one gold, together with a couple of paint brushes. When she'd finished, she stepped back to survey her handiwork. The three of them shook with the effort of trying to suppress their laughter. They didn't want to attract any attention.

The word 'Mr.' had been painted out in black. In gold paint, Angie had painted a capital 'G' in front of Roper. On either side of the writing, she'd painted two little outstretched hands. So, the notice now read, "Reserved for A. GRoper" flanked by two little "wandering hands."

"He never comes in until lunchtime," gasped Angie between giggles. "All the morning shoppers will see it before he gets here and he'll be furious."

The three friends enjoyed the moment, acknowledging that although it was a childish prank, nevertheless, it was fun.   However, it turned out to be a better way of "showing Anthony Roper" than they had ever dreamt of, with long-lasting effects too. For many a year after that evening, the cinema owner was referred to locally as 'Roper the Groper'.

Decisions and Plans

Although Angie was glad to be out of the reaches of Roper the Groper, she was still left with the thorny problem of how she could earn some pocket money for the next few weeks until she'd finished her college course, then be able to apply for a full-time job. She felt confident she'd find something in the short-term, but after that there was the whole question of her future to consider. Did she really want to be a secretary, a typist, or a book keeper? Mrs. Caswell advised her that she would be able to earn good money in that line of work until she got married, after which she would have a husband to look after her. That posed another question for Angie. Did she want to get married? Did she want to be financially dependent on a husband? An article in a national newspaper eventually helped her find the answers, enabling her to reach some major decisions and make firm plans.

The article in question was on the Women's Page, describing how British female secretaries were being eagerly sought after by American companies. They were considered to be highly efficient as well as being a desirable status symbol. Last, but not least, they earned very good salaries.

This was all Angie needed. She felt that life as a secretary in the U.S.A. would tick all the boxes for her. She had no plans for marriage; she longed for her independence in an atmosphere where her skills would be both valued and rewarded. America! It sounded so exciting.

Her decision made, Angie decided to get her plans off the ground by setting up an appointment at the Burlington Recruitment Agency in Wollingford to see how they could help. She explained how she needed a part-time job for a few weeks and that she would like to go and work in America as soon as possible.

She was interviewed by a youngish woman called Helen Grey, to whom she took an immediate liking. After hearing the plan Helen leaned back in her chair, smiling. "You certainly know your own mind, Angie, don't you? Let's go through your plan."

"First of all, how are you doing at college? In all honesty, will you be achieving good results at the end of this term?" Angie assured her that she was one of the top students.

"As well as commercial subjects, do you speak any foreign languages?"

"Yes, I have a high standard of French."

"Do you have a current driving licence?"

"No, but now that I'm seventeen I've just applied for my provisional licence and will be having driving lessons. It's all part of my major plan."

"So far, so good," said Helen. "Now, let me tell you what I think you'll need to do if you really want to carry this through. First of all, the girls who get the top jobs have the top qualifications. You've done well so far, but you need to continue your studies if you want to be up there amongst the best. Also, you need some good secretarial experience. You won't get a top job without it. You'll need references and, I'm sorry to tell you, it's doubtful whether they'll accept anyone under the age of twenty-one. Driving will be useful, as will your French. I must say, I admire your aims. May I make a few suggestions?"

Angie nodded. "I'd be glad of any help or advice you care to give."

"Well, we're fairly new here. We haven't been going long but we certainly haven't let the grass grow under our feet. You're not the only one with ambition around here Angie. We provide both permanent and temporary staff, and have built up a huge customer base which we manage to satisfy successfully. However, by sheer coincidence, we've just been asked to do a job for a small concern that is expanding its services into France. As they need us to translate some of their correspondence, you may be just the one to fit the bill."

"Our reputation for providing only the best staff is absolutely crucial to our success. Therefore, I'll need you to take a short test and if you pass that, then we'll be able to make you an offer. We can provide part-time work here in the office on the translation job until you leave college. After that, I suggest you go onto our temporary staff register. We have enough work to keep you fully occupied and it'll give you a wide work experience. In the future I'll give you an opportunity to decide whether you want to remain as a temp or whether you want to take a permanent job. Meanwhile, continue with your studies at evening classes and by the time you're old enough you'll be ready to apply for one of those plum American jobs. How does that sound?"

Angie could have kissed her, but she restrained herself, took the test and passed with flying colours.

Back home in the stone cottage in Millbeck, she told her mother her plans. "I shall start to save immediately for driving lessons," she announced.

"Why?" asked a puzzled Mrs. Caswell. "You know your father will give you a lift anywhere in the estate van. You just have to ask and he's there."

Angie sighed. "You don't get it, do you Mother? Dad's lovely but I want to be independent. Once I've passed my test I'll save up for a car, then I can go wherever I want whenever I want." Her mother shook her head. "I don't understand you our Angie. You young things nowadays are never satisfied."

A few months later Angie arrived home from work to find a shiny black car parked outside their house. Indoors, she found her father sitting by the fireside, smoking his pipe, reading the newspaper.

"Who's visiting?" she asked.

"No one. Why do you ask?"

"That's a nice car out there and I just put two and two together, but obviously made five."

Just then Mrs. Caswell came bustling into the room, looking unusually excited. "Have you told her Dad? Have you told her about the car?" Without waiting for him to reply, she continued. "Your father's been thinking for some time about buying a family car. We've been fortunate to have the use of the van but we can only use that locally. Now we can go anywhere we want. He's taking me shopping in Wollingford tomorrow and then, guess what; he's taking me to see your Auntie Margaret. She's going to be so surprised to see us turn up in a car." Breathless, she plumped down on the nearest chair, eyes sparkling with anticipation.

Mr. Caswell seized the opportunity to speak. "Seeing as how you've done so well in passing your test, you can borrow the car when you want it Angie. I know you'll be careful." Angie kissed the top of his head. "You're just the best, Dad."

Having transport enabled Angie to muster Dennis and Sandra so that the trusty trio could venture further afield to explore pastures new. Their Sunday car trips became a regular thing, until Sandra fell madly in love with someone called Michael; she seized every possible opportunity to spend time with the extraordinary Michael, including Sunday afternoons. Abandoned for romance, Angie and Dennis continued exploring by car until the estate manager at Holliwell Hall offered Dennis extra work on Sundays, which was a welcome boost to the young man's wages. As it was an offer he couldn't afford to refuse, their Sunday trips petered out to a standstill.

However, Angie was not the only person to have her life transformed by having the use of a car. She was amazed to discover that her stay-at-home mother simply adored going out in the car.   Proudly wearing her 'Sunday best', she'd trot out to the gleaming black car, secretly hoping the neighbours were watching from behind their net curtains. At first, her obliging husband had driven her to visit relatives she hadn't seen for years, but after the novelty of that wore off, the couple, complete with picnic in the boot, enjoyed being weekend tourists, discovering beauty spots and places of interest further afield. Angie was happy for them, especially as she had now lost interest in the car and had resorted to 'borrowing' Samson for company on long walks up on the hills where she had roamed as a young child.

Ambition

For Angie, the time she worked at Burlington Recruitment Agency was a very happy and fulfilling period of her life. The young owners of the company were determined to make a success of their business and created a stimulating, positive atmosphere for their staff. Angie thrived in that environment. She tackled any job that was thrown her way, growing in confidence with every new experience. After working as a temp for a couple of years, Helen offered her a permanent role in the Wollingford office, as a form of promotion. A delighted Angie accepted, setting about learning every aspect of the business.

Shortly after her twentieth birthday, Angie appeared in Helen's office.

"Do you remember when I came for my initial interview, Helen? I told you that my long-term plan was to work in America. You told me then that I should work and learn here in England until I became of age. Well, I've been thinking. It all changed a couple of years ago when they allowed us to vote at the age of eighteen. I'm no longer classed as a minor in this country. Will it be the same in the U.S.A.?"

Helen looked startled. "What's brought this on? I thought you were enjoying your work. We think you're great and wouldn't like to lose you. I rely on you for so many things."

"I love it here and you've been so good to me. It's just that I've always wanted to carry out my original plan. There's a big world out there and I want to see some of it. I shall miss you dreadfully but something inside tells me I should seize the moment. Do you think I'm ready?"

Her friend and mentor thought about it carefully. She was very fond of Angie and valued her contribution to the company. "I'm trying not to be selfish Angie, because I want you to stay here. However, I'll give you my honest opinion. You're a teeny bit young but you're very capable. I'll try my contacts and see if there's anything going that might be of interest to you. Meanwhile, think about presentation."

"What's wrong with my presentation? I thought you were happy with my work."

"No, silly, not your work; your physical presentation. You hope to work in the executive sector of the American business world. You'll find it's a smarter, slicker place than little old Wollingford. You'll need to wear a smart business suit and immaculate shirt. You won't find the businessmen going into the office looking casual. Take a leaf out of their book. Also, you'll need a new hairdo. Smart is the key word."

"Thanks for the advice Helen and for the offer to make enquiries. I really am grateful. I won't let you down."

"One more thing Angie. Get rid of your Derbyshire accent."

"I didn't know I had one. I've always spoken like this."

Helen laughed. "I know you have but you'll have to adapt it. I don't mean you should take on some silly, pretentious way of speaking. Study the newsreaders on the television and see if you can spot any major differences in their pronunciation and your own. BBC English is acceptable anywhere.

Helen was as good as her word. Within weeks, wearing a smart navy suit, crisp white shirt and navy court shoes, and with her hair pinned on top of her head, Angie set out for London for the first time in her young life. The interview Helen had arranged was for a job with an American marketing and recruitment agency in New York. Angie passed with flying colours. They couldn't offer her a job as an executive secretary but felt she had a lot to contribute and would be a useful member of staff. Instead, they offered her a job as a general secretarial help in the main office, bearing in mind her proficiency in French, which they believed could prove useful for special projects. Angie floated home on cloud nine to give the news to her anxiously waiting parents.

"You're going to be a sad miss here," her father told her, "but if it's what you want, then I'm happy for you. Your mother and I never had the chances you young ones have to see the world. Grab your opportunity and enjoy it. If you don't like it, you know where your home is."

Mrs. Caswell was slightly misty-eyed, trying to put on a brave face. "Your dad's right. It's a good chance to see the world and you must take it. Let us have your address and phone number. Keep in regular touch so that we know what's happening. You know I shall worry whatever you do but there's nothing we can do about that. I'm excited and happy for you Angie, but it's certainly a big leap into the dark amongst all those strangers"...

...Angie smiled; she couldn't have wished for better parents. It all seemed so long ago. She became vaguely aware of someone tapping her on the arm. Opening her eyes, she was jolted back to the present by a uniformed air hostess leaning towards her. "Are you alright, madam?" she enquired, with a glance at the sick bag. "Can I get you a drink? We'll be serving food in about five minutes."

Introduction to America

After the food had been cleared away and the stream of passengers strolling round to stretch their legs had subsided, the lights were subdued on the plane. Angie settled down to try to sleep but her thoughts kept wandering back to that first time she had ever flown; that first, scary, exciting trip, all alone on her way to the Big Apple.

It was midday when she landed in New York. She was met by Hal, the company driver, who drove her smoothly, in a huge Chevrolet, through streets crammed with people, street vendors, cars, cabs, and on past the incredibly tall skyscrapers she'd read about in magazines. It was like a dream world; it couldn't be real.

On her arrival Angie was introduced to Ben Hudson, the office manager, who proceeded to explain her duties, introduce her to several other staff members and allocate her a desk. Finally, Ben took her to meet the managing director, Reuben Goldberg.

Reuben was a dignified, quietly-spoken man, greying at the temples. He explained that he liked to meet every member of his staff to make them feel at home and part of the larger team. His eyes twinkled as he explained, "I like them to know that I'm not some fierce dragon up here on the top floor, waiting to pounce on them. Well, not unless they do something stupid." He wished her well and hoped she'd be happy in her work. Angie's head was spinning by this time.

Her first day ended with Hal once more driving her through the crowded city streets to deposit her, together with her luggage, at her new home, an apartment she'd share with five other girls from the company. Exhausted, she made her excuses early in the evening, crawled into her welcoming bed and slept soundly, waking to the sound of her alarm clock next morning, bright-eyed and bushy-tailed, ready to start her new life.

She settled into New York more quickly than she'd imagined. Although the girls at the apartment were a friendly bunch, easy to get along with, the ambitious Angie had other ideas about her accommodation. She still had her mind set firmly on getting to the top of the ladder. In her reckoning, she couldn't see how she could ever be considered as an individual if she was seen as just one of the girls. Within a month she had moved out, on amicable terms, and set up home in her own tiny apartment in a reasonable part of town, wallowing in her precious independence.

The Funeral

Life was good until the day a telephone call from the U.K. changed her life forever. Angie had given her family her office number to be used only in emergencies and so when Carla, one of the switchboard operators, rang through, saying Auntie Margaret was on the phone, Angie's heart sank. Something must be wrong.

Her aunt was phoning to tell her that there had been a terrible accident. Mr. and Mrs. Caswell had been out in the car on one of their little jaunts when a huge transport lorry behind them suffered brake failure. They had died instantly. Angie desperately tried to take in what her aunt was saying. She'd only spoken to her parents a couple of days ago. They were fine then; how could they be dead? It was all too sudden. Had Tony, her brother, been informed? Auntie Margaret told her she was trying to contact Tony, who was abroad with the Army. Also, she asked when Angie would be able to return home to help arrange the funeral and sort out her parents' affairs. Too stunned to weep, a devastated Angie replaced the receiver, sat staring into space in absolute disbelief, then went to find Ben Hudson, the office manager.

Ben was extremely sympathetic and kind. He gave her a coffee and told her to sit quietly in his office while he went off to make arrangements to cover her work in her absence. He returned shortly with a message that Reuben Goldberg wanted to see her up on the fifth floor. A confused Angie duly did as she was bid, wondering why on earth the managing director would need to see her. Would he be cross because she needed time off so soon after joining the company? Would she lose her job? So be it; she would be on the next flight possible, whatever he said.

To her surprise, Reuben's reaction was nothing like she'd imagined. He was very sad for her, saying family was one of the most precious gifts we ever receive in life and their loss brought incomparable sorrow. He'd lost many of his close family members in the Holocaust. Angie finally broke down at this point, weeping inconsolably. Reuben pushed the Kleenex box towards her.

"I don't want you to have any extra worries at this time Angie. I've asked Ben to arrange a return ticket for you to fly back home as soon as possible, at the expense of the company. You haven't been here long but you've certainly made your mark already and you're a valued member of staff. I don't know how long you'll need to be away, but on your return, please make an appointment to come and see me; I have something I want to discuss with you."

Angie didn't stay in the U.K. very long. She arranged the funeral to take place at the village church where her parents were to be buried alongside several of their ancestors. The church was packed and floral tributes covered a huge area of the church yard. Her parents had lived in the village all their lives and were a well-respected part of the community. Angie went through the whole proceedings like a zombie, totally devoid of emotion apart from a gnawing emptiness which was threatening to engulf her. She and Tony clung tightly to each other as the coffins were slowly lowered into the earth.

Afterwards she caught up briefly with Sandra and Dennis, hugged them tightly then stood solemnly by the church gate with Tony to accept the condolences of the many mourners who wanted to express sympathy for their loss. The remainder of her bleak visit was spent in winding up her parents' affairs until, finally, with everything sorted, she returned the keys of the house to the housing manager at Holliwell Hall. Tony had already returned to his Army post and so, grief-stricken, Angie turned her back firmly on the UK. to make her lonely way back to America.

Return to the Home of the Brave

Angie settled into her seat for the return flight to America, in a very different form of mind from that first time when she had set out full of excitement, elated by the thought of what lay ahead. As she sank back wearily, removing her shoes and displaying her sick bag on her lap, she was glad to note that the seat next to her had remained empty even though take-off was close, with air hostesses checking that luggage racks were securely closed and seat belts were being worn. "Great," she thought, "I won't be bothered with chatter and I'll be able to spread out a little." Her heavy eyelids closed.

A welcome drowsiness was beginning to overtake the constant feeling of anxiety and sadness when the sharp snap of the overhead luggage rack awoke her with a jarring jolt. Unfamiliar voices were chatting close-by her seat.

"I'm sorry sir, but this is the only seat we have vacant. The pilot has actually held the flight for you as you're a last-minute booking. Would you like to take your place and put on your seat belt or we'll lose our slot in the take-off queue? We really must get going now."

"I appreciate what you're saying but I genuinely suffer from a phobia. If I don't sit by a window, I have panic attacks during the flight."

The long-suffering hostess leaned over to speak to Angie. With a meaningful look at the sick bag, she asked, "Ma'am, are you O.K. Are you feeling ill? Can I get you anything?"

"No thank you," replied Angie. "I'll be O.K. if I can sit quietly, listening to my music. The bag is just an emergency measure."

"I hope you don't mind my asking you, ma'am, but do you have a strong preference for a window seat? Our friend here has a health problem and needs to sit by a window."

For the first time, Angie looked up at the tall, auburn-haired man at her side. His earnest, blue eyes seemed to bore a hole deep into her consciousness as he pleaded, "I'm sorry to appear so pathetic but the problem is beyond my control. If you wouldn't mind swapping seats with me I promise you faithfully I won't be a scrap of bother for the rest of the flight. I'll be as quiet as a church mouse." The comparison between this large man and a tiny mouse was so ridiculous, it actually raised a smile from Angie. Anyway, who could resist those eyes? She gave him her seat and he was true to his word. After an uneventful flight she was glad to find herself back in the bustle of New York.

Next day, on her return to work, she went to see Reuben Goldberg up on the fifth floor, as he'd requested. It didn't take him long to get down to business.

"I've been keeping an eye on you ever since you joined this company, young lady. I know you're ambitious; I realized that when I first read your job application. I also know you're extremely efficient and reliable. You tackle any task you're given and we can rely on you to carry it out efficiently. I think you're just the person to fill the role which has been created during our recent re-organization discussions."

For the first time since her parents' death, Angie felt a surge of excitement and interest. She leaned forward in her seat, intent on what Reuben was saying.

"We're taking a new approach to the way in which we handle initial contacts. In the past, Ben Hudson allocated the work to whoever was available. We need a more focussed, professional way of handling these contacts. We need a liaison administrator who will meet with every new client to discuss their needs and establish a plan of action. You'll make appointments for them with personnel inside or outside this company, you'll provide them with any necessary information, you'll make sure you're available when they need you and to facilitate all that, you'll be provided with a secretary. You'll guide clients every step of the way so that their requirements are fully met to reach a successful conclusion to their business with this company. You'll have my authority to liaise with any member of staff, whatever their position in this firm. If you have any problems, report back directly to me. Any questions?"

"Why me? I'm a relative newcomer? I don't want to step on anyone's toes."

"The person who fills this demanding post has to be exactly right. I think you're that person. Do you want to give it a try? There's a salary raise involved?"

"It sounds fascinating. In fact, I'd accept the offer even without the salary raise, although it helps."

Reuben smiled. "A word of advice Angie; don't ever say that to anyone again or you'll stay poor for the rest of your life, believe me."

Angie was floating on air. A liaison administrator with her own private secretary. She'd make sure Reuben wouldn't regret the faith he'd placed in her.

That afternoon she received a telephone call from Ben Hudson. "Congratulations Angie. I know you'll do just fine. I'll have an office ready for you tomorrow morning, complete with secretary. Meanwhile, I wonder if you might like to help me with a slight problem I have here. A guy wandered in from the street without an appointment; said we'd been recommended. I could make an appointment for another day or you might like to see him today; he's only in New York for a few days. I don't want to lose him."

"I'll be straight over Ben." As Angie entered his office, Ben stood, gesturing toward a man in a smart, dark suit, seated in front of his desk. "Hi Angie, let me introduce you to another Brit; this is Rob Anderson. As he spoke, the man stood up to face Angie; a flash of recognition streaked across his handsome features. "Ah! It's my saviour, the Sick Bag Lady," he said, holding out his hand. "The Church Mouse, I presume," returned Angie, laughingly, as they shook hands.

Ben looked on, puzzled. "Don't tell me; you two Brits know each other. I hear your country's small, but I didn't realize it was that small."

The ice was broken. Angie's first project as liaison administrator had got off to a good start.

Don't Mix Business with Pleasure

Bearing in mind that Rob Anderson was in the country for only a few days, Angie made an appointment to see him next morning. He arrived bang on time, bearing a document case in one hand and a brown paper bag in the other.

"Good morning, Angie," he beamed. "I hope you don't mind but I've taken the liberty of getting us both a coffee from the corner stand. I've seen them do that in the American movies and I just couldn't resist it."

Rob explained how he was a director of a small, prosperous company in the U.K. that designed and made state-of-the-art jewellery for the rich and trendy. Most of the work consisted of unique pieces made on commission. They wanted to break into the American market and were currently involved in negotiations to buy a long-established family jeweller's business which was up for sale in New York. Rob was fairly sure the deal would go ahead, enabling his current British company to use it as a launching pad to sell their designer jewellery and services in the U.S.A.

They wanted to hit the ground running, so that was why he needed help from Angie to put together a top-class marketing team. Later, they would need help to find the right personnel to staff the new enterprise. This could mean big bucks for Reuben Goldberg's agency; Angie could see dollar signs spinning before her eyes.

They spent most of the morning poring over marketing schemes recently produced by the company to see if any particular style appealed to Rob. After a whole morning of in-depth discussion, he straightened up, stretching his arms sideways. Glancing at his watch, he said, "Are we about done here?"

Angie nodded vigorously. "If you're O.K. with the progress made, I think we should take a break. I'm starving."

Rob looked relieved. "That makes two of us. What do you say if I take us both out to lunch? Can you suggest a good restaurant?"

"That's very kind of you but I'm afraid I can't accept; first, because I'm snowed under with work and should only take a short break, and secondly, because I'm not comfortable about you paying for my lunch. If you're still interested in the American experience, how about the diner round the corner where we can go halves? It's quick, cheap and cheerful; it also means we can get back here to make some more progress on your project before you return to the U.K.

They worked all afternoon, then continued next morning. After Rob picked out a couple of marketing schemes that appealed to him, Angie introduced him to the two men responsible for them, who in turn promised to draft a few ideas based on Rob's description of what he needed. Between them Angie and Rob had covered a lot of ground in only a couple of days.

Back in her office, Angie held out her hand. "I think we've got the work off to a good start, don't you? The guys sound interested and will come up with some great ideas for you. Let me know when you plan to return to New York and we'll meet up again to find the best way of moving forward. Safe journey, and I hope you get a window seat."

"Ouch!" he grinned. "I think you've covered an amazing amount of ground, considering the time available. To show my appreciation, and as it's my last evening, why don't you let me take you out to dinner, unless you have other plans? I'll be all on my lonesome otherwise."

"That's a sad picture you conjure up but I'm afraid I'm not able to take you up on your generous offer. I never mix business with pleasure. Thank you, all the same."

Rob put on his hang-dog look. "That's a shame. I wasn't thinking of mixing them; we won't discuss business, we'll just make it pure pleasure."

With a twinge of regret, Angie turned down the invitation. She liked this man; there was something wholesome about him that appealed to her. However, she loved her job too much to become socially involved with a client. Keep life simple; the golden rule.

During the next six weeks, Rob had made a further two visits to the States. Angie liaised successfully between him and various members of staff. She also helped him with his queries regarding external services to help him find his feet in a strange country until she felt he'd got his project off the ground and there was no need for her particular services at this stage of his plans. Accordingly, she handed him on to her colleagues, telling him to contact her if she could ever be of further help. She was pleasantly surprised, therefore, when, on his next visit, she found him standing in front of her desk again.

"I suppose if I ask you to go to lunch with me at the diner today, you'll refuse because we aren't officially working together at the moment. You'll send me away to have lunch with the guys."

"You've got it. It's a sad world isn't it?"

"O.K. I know you'll be happy to hear that work with the guys is going very well and we're getting along just fine. However, there's something else that I need to discuss with you, besides lunch. We've managed to close the deal with the jewellery company but there are still a few details to sort out before we can open at their old premises. In the meantime, as part of our pre-opening marketing campaign, I need to rent gallery space to mount an exhibition to let people know what we're all about and that we'll shortly be opening right here, in the Big Apple. Can you help?"

"I've appointments all morning but I'll meet you at the diner for lunch to discuss your requirements. This afternoon, I'll get on to the property realtors to search for suitable premises. Then, we'll take it from there."

Angie was delighted at the prospect of working with Rob for a little longer. Although there was no shortage of clients to keep her busy, none were quite like this affable Brit. She loved the easy rapport that had built up between the two of them and began to look forward to his visits. Thinly disguised as a joke, he repeatedly invited her to keep him company during his lonely stays in New York but, apart from lunch at the local diner, Angie was determined to keep business and pleasure separate.

Gradually, she was developing a social life in her new situation. Colleagues often invited her to barbecues or dinner parties. Sometimes they tried to team her up with their eligible bachelor friends but Angie was more interested in her career than romance and managed to keep them at arm's length while still remaining the popular, sociable, British girl that everyone liked to have around. She enjoyed joining them in supporting the local baseball team, learned how to play ten pin bowling with them and then, one day, completely on a whim, she bought herself a bicycle. Angie loved cycling round the park on her own. It wasn't quite the same as exploring with Sandra and Dennis, but she enjoyed the physical activity and it was a way of being part of the American scene without always having to be involved in invitations. She tried hard to forget the recent sadness she'd left behind in the U.K. and threw herself whole-heartedly into her new lifestyle.

The exhibition that Rob had mentioned took up much more of her time than she had at first imagined. Initially, she found various properties for him to view. Once he'd chosen the most suitable premises for an exhibition he returned to ask for help in finding builders, electricians and decorators to make minor adjustments and improvements. Although this wasn't usually within Angie's remit, she helped him as he was one of their potentially valuable clients and also, being a stranger in a foreign land, he was unsure of whom to contact. Once that had been achieved, he asked for help in finding the right staff to help man the exhibition, help with invitations and so it continued; every time Angie thought her involvement had ended, Rob asked for more help. The weeks and months flew by until eventually everything was in place and ready to roll.

Angie had enjoyed the project more than she'd realized and found she had mixed feelings about the accomplishment. She thrived on the stimulus of helping get everything organized and was proud of the end result, but, at the same time, was sorry there was no more need for her services. Also, Rob had been spending increasing amounts of time in New York. Angie enjoyed working with him and had got used to him being around; that would now stop, although he would continue to work with the marketing guys in the office.

"Two days to go until the occasion of the year," he remarked cheerfully as he flopped into one of her office chairs.

"I'm sure it will run like clockwork, without a hitch," she replied. "You seem to have covered every eventuality. Everyone will have a wonderful time and you'll get loads of business from it. Just you wait and see. I'll be thinking of you."

"Aren't you coming?"

"Well, no. This is about reaching out to your customer base. My work is finished. The rest is up to you and your team."

Rob looked stunned. "I don't believe this. After all the work you've put in, aren't you just a little bit curious as to how it will all pan out?"

"Well, yes, but ..."

"But nothing, and don't try to give me your usual spiel about business and pleasure. The evening won't be complete without your presence. Cancel whatever you've got planned and come. Please, Angie."

"O.K. I'd love to come really but you hadn't mentioned anything and I didn't like to be pushy."

Rob threw his head back and roared with laughter. "You're a strange one Angie Caswell."

The Exhibition

Angie took one last look in the mirror. This was a very important occasion for Rob and she couldn't let him down. That's what she told herself but in reality it was an important event for her, even though she was feeling very confused about it. She couldn't decide whether her attendance at the exhibition was a social or business occasion. Usually she was dressed in formal, business attire when she saw Rob but the invitation cards she'd seen specifically stated cocktail dresses and lounge suits. She'd decided to go with the cocktail dress but, unusually for her, she felt a little nervous. A ring at the door spurred her into action. It was Brian, her local taxi driver. No more time for worrying, this was it.

As she entered the gallery Angie was struck by the heavy scent of expensive perfume hanging on the warm air and the hum of polite conversation. She paused in the doorway, a vision of elegance in a stylish, midnight blue, brocade dress and matching jacket with stand-away collar and three-quarter length sleeves. Her blonde curls cascaded freely around her shoulders in sharp contrast to the dark hue of her jacket. Rob spotted her immediately and came hurrying over. As he approached he opened his eyes wide, pursing his lips in a silent gesture of admiration.

"Is this the Angie Caswell I thought I knew so well? You look absolutely fabulous. Let me introduce you to a few people. Come and meet Dolores." He walked over to a small group of guests with champagne glasses in their hands.

"Dolores, meet Angie, my right hand man in tonight's event. Angie, this is Dolores Valanquez."

Dolores was a tall, curvy woman with jet black hair piled high on her head and a slightly haughty air about her.

"Good to meet you, dear. So, you're Rob's secretary? Lucky girl." Dolores flashed Rob an intimate glance from under her long, dark lashes.

Angie felt a twinge of irritation but disguised it in a friendly smile. "No, it's quite the reverse; Rob is actually the lucky one to have me," she said, exchanging a cheeky grin with him. "I'm an extremely busy liaison administrator with a top-class American agency. Actually, here's my card. Should you ever find you need my services, just ring this number and my secretary will be pleased to make an appointment. May I ask what you do, Dolores?"

"Do? My father's in oil; you've probably heard of him."

Smiling sweetly, Angie continued, "My father was in gardening but I chose not to follow him. Did you follow your father into oil?"

This produced a deep, throaty laugh from Dolores. "No, honey, I'm too busy spending his money to follow him anywhere."

Unabashed, Angie went on to say, "Long may it last. I'm sure you won't mind my being a little personal, but I have to tell you, Dolores, I adore your dress. Prada, isn't it? As for that little Lieber bag, it's to die for isn't it?"

Angie had recognized Dolores' vain streak and was pressing all the right buttons. Lapping it up, Dolores tossed her head slightly, fingering the dazzling array of diamonds around her neck.

"An heirloom?" queried Angie. "That's magnificent."

"How did you guess? It was my paternal grandmother's."

"Well, I guessed because everything about you screams 'modern woman' but your lovely diamonds are in a vintage setting. Have you ever considered having them re-styled to bring them in line with your very obvious taste for everything the current top designers can dream up? I'll bet Rob and his team would love to work on stones of that quality. They'd be able to create something exquisite which would be unique to just little old you."

Rob had stood quietly watching the interchange between the two women, wearing a polite, slightly amused expression on his face. As Angie paused, he was right on cue.

"There's absolutely no doubt about the quality of those diamonds. Would you like me to introduce you to our design team, Dolores? I'm sure they'd love to see your beautiful jewellery. Would you excuse us, Angie? I'll be back."

As she slowly made her way over to where drinks were being served, Angie paused to look at an exhibit. A voice in her ear remarked, "Somebody has one fabulous imagination, don't they? They've produced some most unusual pieces."

Angie turned to see a pleasant, middle-aged man, gesturing towards the exhibit. "I think they're definitely some of the big names of the future," she replied.

"Oh, you're from England! I just love your accent. Say something else to me."

"Would you excuse me, please? There's someone waiting for me over there." Angie moved on towards a well-earned drink. Along the way, several people spoke to her, several of them interested in her English accent. One extremely friendly lady told her, "I have a friend in Bristol, England. Her name is Elizabeth Thompson. Do you know her?"

Time dragged for Angie. She'd looked around the exhibition. She'd made conversation with several people. She was rapidly becoming very bored. Every time she looked over towards Rob he seemed to be engrossed in conversation with some woman or other. Also, the alcohol consumption in the room was beginning to influence the ever-increasing sound level. She'd had enough. Decision made, Angie made her way to the exit. Just as she reached the door a breathless Rob rushed towards her. "You're not leaving are you?" he asked. "I've hardly seen you."

"I didn't think you'd notice in the general rush to grab your attention. Your exhibition is a smash hit; well done."

"Yes, and it's all your doing. As soon as the word got out that Dolores Valanquez had given us a commission, every man and his wife decided they must do the same. You started the ball rolling and it shows no sign of stopping."

"I'm really pleased for you Rob. Honestly, I am, but there's no point in my hanging around. I've had a good look at everything. Thanks for the invite, now I'll be on my way. See you around."

Rob stepped forward to place his hand gently on her arm. "Please do one more thing for me Angie. I wanted to show you something special this evening. I'll be so disappointed if my plan falls through. Can you hang on while I have a quick word with my secretary, then I'll be straight back to you?"

"You have five minutes max. before I make a break for it. I can't stand any more of this crazy crowd."

True to his word, Rob left the excitement of the exhibition to lead a curious Angie out to a waiting cab. "Where are we going?" she enquired.

"Sit back and relax. You'll find out soon enough. I can tell you, though, I think it's somewhere you've never been before."

The taxi cab came to a halt in front of a smart apartment block called 'Athenium Heights'. "What are we doing here? Do you know someone? I thought you wanted to show me something?" Rob laughed as he offered his hand to help her out of the cab. "Do you ever relax?" he asked. "Stop asking questions just for a few minutes at least and follow me."

He led her through the smartly appointed lobby to the elevator, taking her up to the top floor. Pulling out a key from his pocket, he threw open the door and, with an expansive sweep of his arm, said, "Welcome to my new abode."

Angie was quite taken aback when she stepped inside. "This is luxury Rob. I love it. I especially love these floor-to-ceiling windows; you can see all of New York from here."

"Not quite, but it's not bad is it?"

"Not bad? Look at this bathroom; you could hold a party in it, there's so much space. Oh! Look at your music system. That's just something else! Have you got any music to play on it?"

"I'm afraid there's not much of a selection. I need to do something about that but I'll play what's here." The sounds of Duke Ellington drifted out of speakers strategically placed around the room. A delighted Angie watched as he walked over towards the light switches near the door, saying, "And for my next trick ..." The lights dimmed to an intimate glow.

"May I have this dance, Miss Caswell?"

"I thought you'd never ask, Mr. Anderson."

They joked and chatted as they danced around the room, then a silence fell over them, a comfortable silence. There was no need to talk, being close, with the soft music as a background, was enough. When he held her closer, she happily melted against him, both dancers hoping this magical mood would never end.

When the music eventually stopped Angie threw off her high-heeled shoes and flopped onto a comfy sofa, beside Rob. "Were you joking about this being your new abode? Is it really yours or have you borrowed it from a friend?"

"Here we go, the grand inquisition. It's mine and if you need absolute proof, I can show you the papers I signed with the agent yesterday."

"Are you coming to live in America then?"

"Yes and no. My main home will still be in England but I shall be spending increasing amounts of time in New York so it seems to make sense that I have a comfortable pad over here. I wanted to show it to you because I feel it needs a woman's touch to make it a real home from home. If you're not doing anything tomorrow, I wondered if you might like to go shopping with me to buy some home comforts, with music being top of the list of course."

"I'd love to do that. What time did you have in mind and where do you want to meet?" Angie leaned forward to put on her shoes.

"What are you doing? I liked it when you made yourself comfy."

"I'm going home of course. I'll meet you tomorrow to help you with your shopping. Thank you for showing me your apartment. It's lovely."

Rob stared at her in absolute amazement. "I just don't get you Angie. I thought you were having a good time. It's great being with you for 'pleasure' instead of 'business'. You look so lovely this evening; in fact, you were the most gorgeous woman in the room. I could see women looking at you with envy and I can only describe the look in the men's eyes as lust." Angie stared back in disbelief.

"The night is young; too young for you to take off your glad rags to curl up with a book in front of the fire. I've found a smooth club round the corner from here which I think you might like. We could have dinner, enjoy the cabaret and even have another dance. I'd love to take you and show you off to the whole of the Big Apple. What d'you say?"

Secretly, Angie was delighted. She'd been unimaginably happy, snuggled up to Rob, dancing around the room. When he began to discuss shopping, her previous confusion had returned; had things suddenly changed back from pleasure to business? "I'll bet you say that to all the girls," she said, trying to hide her true feelings. "The club sounds like the place to be, so how can I refuse an offer like that. Let's do it."

"Thank goodness for that," grinned Rob. "I took the liberty of booking a table for us."

Getting to Know You

The waiter showed them to a candlelit table to the side of the small dance floor. Rob and Angie studied the huge, leather-bound menus against a background of a piano softly tinkling, accompanied by the deep, rhythmic sounds of the double bass.

"Tonight's a special night; the first time out together socially. Would you like to celebrate with champagne?"

Angie shook her blonde curls. "I don't really go a bundle on champagne. It seems to me that people have champagne when they want to make an impression. I hope you don't mind but I'd rather have wine and something to eat. I'm starving."

"O.K. You certainly come right out and say it like it is. I'll stop trying to impress you. To be perfectly honest, I'd prefer food. Let's see what they have to offer."

They were part-way through their meal when Rob said, "I have something to confess to you Angie. I hope you're going to be O.K. about it."

For some inexplicable reason, Angie's heart began to thump and her palms were perspiring heavily. "Out with it. I've just settled in to have an extraordinary time with you; don't tell me you're going to wreck it."

"The truth is;" he paused. "I won't be working with you anymore now that my work with you is finished." Angie looked at him uncertainly, wondering exactly what he was trying to tell her."

"Go on," she said. "What are you saying?"

"I'm saying that I prefer pleasure to business when I'm with you Angie Caswell. After all these months, I'm so happy I can now work with just the marketing guys at your office as I no longer need your services. You know what that means, don't you? I can ask you out on dates and you won't be able to give me all that stuff about being a business client. We're free. What are you doing tomorrow, and the day after, and the day after?"

Angie breathed a huge sigh of relief. "That was a rotten trick to play on me. I was worried that you were going to tell me something terrible. I think to make up for that, you should refill our wine glasses and we'll drink a toast to pleasure."

The evening flew by like a dream. The food was delicious, the wine flowed and the cabaret was top class. Rob held Angie's hand as they walked out to the dance floor, then as the evening progressed he put his arm around her shoulders to guide her back to the table. A comfortable, natural closeness had developed between them. The time was approaching midnight when Angie looked at her watch. "I didn't realize it was so late. Is there a telephone," she asked. "I must ring Brian."

"Who's Brian?"

"No one you need to know about."

"Stop being a tease. I feel a need to know about every man in your life. Come on, who is he?"

"Takes a tease to know a tease! Brian is a cab driver who lives in my block. Whenever I need a cab I give him a ring, especially when it's late."

"Touché."

Telephone call made, Rob and Angie awaited his arrival out in the cool of the evening air. Putting his arm around her, he asked, "Did you enjoy this evening as much as I did because for me, it was everything I had hoped it would be and more. You're beautiful Angie, you're wonderful and I want to see you again and again."

For once, Angie didn't try to disguise her feelings. "It was magical Rob. I've loved every minute I was with you. I can't wait to do it again."

He turned her to face him. "So, do I get a goodnight kiss just to make sure you mean what you say?"

"Sure you do," she said, standing on tiptoe to fling both arms around his neck then kissed him fully on the lips.

The sound of Brian's horn brought them both back down to earth. With a promise to meet again next day to go shopping, Angie floated home in an ecstatic whirl. She knew, deep down, that she'd been trying to suppress her feelings towards Rob, just in case they weren't returned. She hadn't dared hope that it would all turn out more gloriously, wonderfully, deliriously than she could ever imagine; she was fast running out of superlatives to describe it. The world was a fabulous place, so full of joy. It took a long time for her to get off to sleep that night, with her mind constantly replaying every second of the evening. Finally, exhausted, she fell into a blissful sleep, happily anticipating a shopping trip with Rob. Shopping had never been her favourite activity but with Rob, it would be different."

They met next day, as planned. The busy streets were bustling with crowds of Saturday shoppers but, cocooned in their own, private, little world, the two were blissfully oblivious of anyone else. They shopped all morning, stopping only to share a lunch, then they shopped all afternoon, eventually staggering into the apartment with arms full of bags and packages. Angie was right; she'd never had so much fun shopping.

They unpacked their parcels like a couple of children on Christmas morning. Each cup, plate, towel and cushion was meticulously put in place, then, deeply satisfied with themselves, they sat back to enjoy the effect of the day's efforts.

"Music or food?" asked Rob, "although I think I can guess what you're going to say."

"Both. I'm starving but we can try some of the new music cassettes while we cook." Enjoying the novelty of the situation, they cooked their first meal together, singing along with favourites from the likes of Stevie

Wonder, Barbra Streisand and the Bee Gees, to name but a few.

As another intimate evening was drawing to a close Rob turned to Angie. "D'you have to go home? After all today's efforts, can't you stay and enjoy everything we've created here between us? I'm already missing you."

Angie struggled to reply. "That's a very tempting offer but I think, perhaps, this is all moving too fast for me to keep up; I'd better give Brian a ring. Besides, I always go cycling in Central Park on a Sunday morning. How d'you amuse yourself on a Sunday?"

"When I'm in New York I usually go to Mass then spend the rest of the day working."

"You're Roman Catholic then?"

"Yes, aren't you?"

"Anglican but I've been struggling with the whole thing recently so let's not talk about it. There's Brian." With a quick kiss, she was gone.

Sunday, Funday

Angie was just going out of the door when the phone rang. "Thought I might have missed you," said Rob's voice at the other end of the line. "Are you still planning to go cycling?"

"I was just leaving. Why?"

"I've managed to borrow a bike from the janitor. I'll see you near the Children's Zoo in fifteen minutes." That was the start of another memorable day for the pair.

They enjoyed a leisurely ride around the park, stopping occasionally to watch the ducks or to buy refreshments. Sitting on a bench, watching the world go by, Rob remarked, "I haven't had this much fun in years. It's like entering another world, watching New York from a bicycle saddle. It's a great idea. Have you any more good ideas for the rest of the day?"

"I'm full of them but, guess what..."

"You're starving."

"Spot on. Let's go to Mike's for lunch, but first we drop our cycles off at my place."

"Is this some subversive plan of yours to lure me into your love nest?"

"No. Sorry to disappoint you. It's purely practical because Mike runs an Irish pub where you might arrive quite safely on a bicycle but leaving on one can be problematic; some might even call it hilarious. Keep with me and I'll guarantee you a fun day."

Having left their bikes at Angie's place, they set out to walk the three blocks to Mike Malone's pub. Painted in emerald green with a huge, illuminated sign in the shape of a shamrock, there was no mistaking the Irish theme. Inside, behind the long bar, stood a heavily built man with a good humoured, rosy face and sparkling blue eyes.

"Well, the saints be blessed, it's Angie and aren't I just after asking Brian if he's set eyes on you lately? You'll be having a Guinness will you? And your friend? Has he developed a taste for the black stuff yet?"

"It's good to see you Mike. This is my friend Rob and if he hasn't tried your stout, then I think he should start right now. That'll be two pints please; we've been cycling and developed a thirst. We're also starving. What can you do about that?"

"You've chosen a grand day to visit us Angie. Patrick O'Halloran has family over on vacation from the home country so we're preparing for a ceilidh and isn't this the band right now?" A lively group of musicians walked through, laughing and chatting while they set up their instruments in the corner of the long room. "It's going to be a day to remember but it does mean that for lunch, the kitchen's having to offer a restricted menu. We have steak and fries, and we can also recommend our fries and steak. I can promise you on my honour that what we lack in variety we more than make up for in flavour." He paused, looking at them expectantly, beaming all over his Irish face.

"Just what we fancied. We'll have one of each."

Several hours and many pints of stout later, Angie and Rob exchanged happy grins. They both agreed it was time they made their way home. Earlier, while they were tucking into their steak and fries, the fiddler began to play and people from all over the area poured into Mike's bar to take part in the ceilidh. The musicians soon got everyone's toes tapping and then when their lead tenor sang "Danny Boy" an amazing hush came over the entire rowdy room. Everyone listened intently, with eyes glistening and a lump in their throats. The tumultuous applause when he'd finished nearly brought the house down and, predictably, when he invited the crowd to join in one more verse with him they all sang with gusto, including Angie and Rob. Later, trays piled high with food were passed around the room, while the beloved black stuff flowed ceaselessly. There was no sign of any of the music, dancing or general celebrations coming to a halt as Angie and Rob prepared to make their departure. The Irish fraternity was set to do Patrick O'Halloran and his family proud.

It was about seven o'clock when Angie and Rob eventually stumbled out of the pub, glad that they'd left their bikes at home.

"I wouldn't have missed that for the world," laughed Rob. "You do realize how you've completely led me astray today; I haven't even been to Mass. Have you got any more ideas?"

"I think you'll like this one. How about if we take a cab to your place; not Brian's cab because he's hardly in any fit state to be driving today. We can listen to some of your music, then, when we've relaxed a bit, you can lead me astray? What d'you say?"

Rob was already hailing a cab.

Back at his apartment, Angie lounged on the sofa while Rob chose the music.

"I can't hear it," she complained.

"Come with me if you want to hear it." He led her into his sumptuous bedroom, where the music was being piped through from the music centre in the lounge. "What could be better?" He dimmed the lights, kissing her unruly curls as they snuggled up together on the luxurious new bedding, relaxing in the romantic atmosphere. She murmured in his ear, "Isn't it wonderful being led astray?"

The music had stopped when Rob awoke to reach out his hand towards his small alarm clock. His movement roused Angie. "What time is it? I think we dozed off."

"It was more than a doze," came the reply. "It's almost 2 o'clock."

"What?" shrieked Angie sitting bolt upright. "Where are my shoes?" She began to tidy her hair and look for her shoes.

"Stay," invited Rob, collapsing back onto the pillows. It's not so comfy here without you."

"Sorry, but I need a cab. I have work tomorrow. I guess we missed our grand finale; that's what too much stout does for you. Shame! What're you doing this evening? We could always pick up where we left off."

Mike Malone got it right; it had indeed been a grand day.

The Telephone Call

For Angie, the next two and a half years were incredibly happy. She had never imagined life could be so wonderful. She loved her job, where she was an increasingly valued member of the company, and she was wholly, madly, ecstatically in love with Rob, who was spending progressively longer periods in New York. Angie chose to maintain a certain amount of independence by keeping her own small apartment, but when Rob was in town she stayed with him. Their living arrangements had just evolved as their relationship grew. There was no need for deep discussion, everything grew from the harmony of their love for each other.

Rob had asked her just once, "I know you lived in England most of your life Angie, but you've never told me whereabouts that was. In fact, I know nothing about you except that I can't live without you."

"Don't ask or you'll spoil everything. I've never asked you anything about your past because I don't want to know. Our past started the day we met. Nothing before that matters because we weren't together. We are who we are now." She looked at his face for a reaction. "Don't worry," she continued, "I don't have any murky skeletons in my cupboard. It's just as I say; life started in earnest when I met you. You are my everything." She hugged him tightly and the subject was never mentioned again. There was no need to refer to it; they were both happy to accept each other for who they were.

One Wednesday evening Angie arrived at Rob's apartment bursting with excitement. She was dying to tell him her life-changing news. Rob was waiting for her, with a bottle of wine and two glasses. Before she could speak, he gave her a big hug and a kiss then said, "If you're wondering why the wine, it's because I've something to tell you this evening but before I start on that, I have a little something to give you. Hang on a minute while I go and fetch it." He went off in the direction of the bedroom.

Angie decided to humour him because whatever he was about to tell her, it couldn't possibly top what she was planning to announce. She was about to pour the wine when the telephone rang. After letting it ring a couple of times, she picked it up, saying "Rob Anderson's phone. Can I help you?" A female voice at the other end asked, "Is Robert there, please?"

"Robert? Oh, you mean..." Before she could finish, the phone was snatched from her grasp. "Hello, Robert here. Is everything O.K.?" Pause. "Someone from work." Pause. "Brought some urgent papers round." Pause. "No, they're for me to work on." Pause. "The airport? Now? You know I don't have a car here. You'll have to grab a cab and I'll see you in half an hour or so." As he turned to face Angie, she saw he had turned as white as a sheet.

"What's happened?" she asked. "Who was that?"

"It's my, erm, my mother. She's on her way here. Never said a dickie bird about it beforehand. Just arrives here like a bolt out of the blue. Drat, drat, drat and DRAT. Why today of all days? I'm truly sorry, Angie, but I shall have to ask you to leave. I can't have a female in the apartment when she arrives."

"What? Why can't I meet her?"

"You don't know my mother. She's a staunch Roman Catholic with very extreme views on relationships and behaviour in general. She can also be most unpleasant." He'd started to tidy away the wine and glasses.

"We'll have to get a move on or she'll be here. I'll ring Brian to collect you while you remove your things from the bedroom and the bathroom." He was looking around distractedly. "I don't think there's anything else of yours around the place but I'll make a quick check. I'm so very sorry, darling. I'll make it up to you, I promise. I love you and upsetting you is the last thing in the world I'd ever do. I understand that this is a big ask, but if you knew the circumstances you'd realize why I have no alternative." He was rushing around looking for evidence of Angie's presence, repeating over and over, "Why tonight of all nights? Why tonight?"

Angie was stunned. She'd never seen her calm, rational partner in such a panic. This mother of his must be quite a piece of work. It would be pointless trying to reason with him while he was in such a disturbed state, so she did as she was bid and piled all her belongings into Brian's cab and kissed Rob goodbye. "I'll give you a ring," he promised as he hared back into the apartment to check that all was as it should be.

Brian looked at the bags piled into the back of his cab, then looked at Angie, one eyebrow raised in query. "Don't ask," she muttered, rolling her eyes. "Would I?" was the quick reply. "Just park-up further down the street, out of the light," she instructed her obliging friend. "I want to see what this fire-breathing mother is like."

They didn't have long to wait until a yellow cab rolled up in front of the apartments. As Rob dashed down the steps, a smartly dressed woman with dark, shoulder-length hair stepped out onto the sidewalk. Rob kissed her on the cheek, picked up her suitcase, then the two of them disappeared through the big glass doors.

"I never saw her face," said Angie, "but did that look like a mother to you Brian?"

"Will you be wanting the Irish answer or the truth?"

"You saw her as well as I did; what d'you think?"

"Perhaps she was a child bride? I've heard of such things."

"Oh, yeah. By my reckoning she must have given birth when she was something like five years old. Take me home, please, Brian. I've no doubt Rob will give me the full story tomorrow."

Angie couldn't get the incident out of her head. The woman obviously wasn't his mother, so who was she? Could she be his step-mother? Perhaps his father had married for a second time to a woman several years his junior? Why was Rob so distraught? She knew nothing about his past so she would have to trust what she did know about him. He'd give her a simple explanation tomorrow morning when he telephoned her. Despite all the sensible reassurances she repeated to herself again and again, she had an uneasy feeling which she couldn't dispel.

After a restless night with only fitful bursts of slumber, Angie dragged herself into work next morning, to wait for Rob's telephone daily call. By mid-day she could stand the suspense no longer so she rang his office, avoiding his home telephone in case "the monster" was still in residence. Patty, Rob's secretary whom Angie had grown to know quite well, answered the phone. "Hi Angie, I'm sorry but Rob's not in today."

"Can you tell me where I can get hold of him Patty?"

"I'm not exactly sure. He's had a family emergency. His wife's over here and I believe they've gone up-state, possibly for a couple of days."

"His wife? Don't you mean his mother?"

"No, I mean his wife."

There was a long pause as Angie struggled to overcome the dizziness which was threatening to overcome her. "His wife," she said weakly, then she heard her own voice emanating from some distant place, becoming increasingly shrill as she repeated, "His wife. Not his mother. His wife. His wife?"

Patty sounded concerned. "Uh, oh, Angie. Didn't you know Rob was married?"

Fighting back the tears, Angie managed to reply, "No. I never asked and he never told me. I just assumed... Why didn't anybody tell me?"

"It's no secret here in the company. Everybody knows. I guessed you'd know too. I'm genuinely sorry you've found out like this. You, more than anybody, must know Rob's a real nice guy, wild about you, and I'm sure he'll explain everything when he gets back. Do me a favour, Angie; please don't tell him I'm the one who let you know. Shall I tell him you phoned?"

"I don't know. Please yourself," murmured Angie as she replaced the receiver. She sat staring into space, trying to make sense of recent events. After a while, she picked up her bag and wandered out to where her secretary, Lana, was working at her desk.

"I'm not feeling 100% today Lana. I'm going home so if anything urgent crops up you can find me there."

Lana looked at her closely; Angie taking time off for sickness was a totally new phenomenon. "You certainly don't look your usual self. I'm ringing a cab; I won't let you make your own way home in that state."

Back in the solitude of her own small apartment, Angie waited for a call, while at the same time going over and over the same old questions in her mind. Why hadn't he told her he was married? Would she have still fallen in love with him had she known about his wife? How long had he been married? Did he have any children? Was he still in love with his wife? The questions spun endlessly in her poor, aching head without the relief of any answers. She tried Rob's phone several times without success. It was one of the longest, dreariest days of her life, which, when dusk fell, found Angie still waiting motionlessly by the telephone, gazing out over the darkening street scene. She'd had neither food nor drink since early morning. Eventually, she snapped, and the relentless questioning turned to a burning anger. She screamed and she sobbed, calling Rob every foul name she could think of for putting her through such anguish. Anything that came to hand was slung across the room in fury. Finally, totally physically and emotionally exhausted, Angie collapsed on her bed fully dressed, pulled up a blanket and dropped into a deep, dark sleep.

Next morning found her feeling a little better for the benefit of a good night's sleep, but still aware of an aching numbness in her head. She went into the office first thing and immediately rang Reuben Goldberg who told her he was free to see her immediately if she'd like to make her way up to his office.

As she walked through the door, he looked up, full of concern. "I heard you went home sick yesterday. How are you today? Better I hope?"

"A little, thanks, Reuben." Angie slumped wearily into one his armchairs.

Reuben looked at her closely. "You don't look your usual self Angie. I know you well enough to tell when something's wrong. What is it?"

It was no surprise to him when Angie told him about her affair with Rob. However, he did raise his eyebrows a little when she told him about the events of the last couple of days.

"He's always struck me as a very pleasant, likeable kind of guy, someone you'd take on trust, so I don't suppose you ever felt the need to ask if was married. Any normal person would just make the assumption, otherwise we'd spend our lives in a permanent state of suspicion and mistrust. There's probably a very reasonable explanation; perhaps this woman is his ex-wife. Are you sure you're not over-reacting?"

"I haven't told you the full story yet. First of all, Rob always rings me at least once every single day so it's most unusual for me not to hear a single word since Wednesday evening. Secondly, I'm pregnant."

"Does he know you're pregnant?"

"He kind of knows. We had our suspicions and I had it confirmed by a doctor on Wednesday. I was all set to tell him the news that evening when the bombshell hit and I was bundled out, lock, stock and barrel. I thought he would be delighted about having a baby but perhaps I'm wrong. Maybe he can't face being a father and that's why he's up-state with some other woman. How could I have got everything so wrong?" The tears started to roll down her cheeks.

"It's never as bad as it seems," comforted the kindly Reuben. "Let's talk it through. When is your baby due?"

"I'm only a few weeks gone, so there's several months to go yet."

"Are you happy about having this baby?"

"I was so excited but now I'm just not sure about anything. If Rob doesn't come back our baby will have no father, but if he does come back, will I be able to trust him again if it's true about him being married? That wouldn't be an ideal atmosphere in which to raise a young child, would it? Also, if I'm on my own, I shall need to earn money to live. How can I work and look after a baby? I'm all mixed up. You're so kind to listen to all my troubles, Reuben. I didn't mean to get so emotional."

"Don't you worry. I hope you know you can always come to me to talk things over. You know Angie, despite your problems, you're a very fortunate young woman. A child is a very precious gift from God. Whatever the circumstances, treasure that gift."

Angie dried her eyes. "I do want this baby really. I just have to figure out how I'm going to manage all on my own. Somehow, I'll find a way because I know Rob's not coming back. I'll just have to give this baby enough love for two."

Reuben gave her a broad, encouraging smile. "That's the way. I'm so proud of you. There's just one thing that slightly concerns me though. You keep repeating that Rob's not coming back. How can you be so sure when you've had such a happy relationship? He's only been gone for two days and none of us know the full details of his situation. Are you sure you're not being a bit hasty? Don't act in haste Angie."

"What you don't know, Reuben, is that when I first met Rob I liked him but I wouldn't date him until my work with him was completed. I was absolutely fastidious about not mixing business with pleasure. Having been so self-disciplined on that issue, I've examined my conscience closely over the past couple of days and I know in my heart of hearts that I wouldn't ever have started anything with him if I'd known he was married. I just wouldn't have got involved. He probably knows that too and that's why he never revealed the whole truth. He did love me but how can I ever trust him again? If we got back together I'd always be wondering if he were being completely honest with me. It's over. It was wonderful while it lasted, but there's someone else I have to consider now."

Reuben gave a half laugh. "Why is it I'm not surprised at your attitude. You've always been one to know your own mind and that's what I like about you. Now, I have a suggestion which you can accept or refuse; it's your choice. My proposal is that you take a year out of work, with full salary, to take some of the pressure off you while you sort out your life. If you want to come back here at the end of the year, we'll have a job for you."

Angie gasped. "You're an angel Reuben, but what about my job? Who's going to take it over?"

"Do you think Lana is ready to take it on if we give her plenty of support? If you could spend some time this coming weekend writing a job resumé together with all the helpful information you can muster, you could start your year's sabbatical on Monday. What d'you think?"

"It sounds absolutely incredible. I'll miss my job and all my friends here but, at the same time, I know I'll be having to make lots of changes in my lifestyle. Having some free time to get everything sorted out will be wonderful." Angie paused. "I don't think I want to stay in my current apartment because I need to make a clean break; I should move on until I've made firm decisions about the future. However, wherever I go, I'll give you a telephone number so that you always know how to contact me. One thing; please keep it a secret. I don't want anyone but you to know my whereabouts."

"Agreed," nodded Reuben. "There's one more thing I need from you Angie. For the time being, I'd like you to ring me once a week otherwise I shall worry about you. Call under a false name if you want to keep your secret, but please keep in touch."

"Of course; I shall call myself Esther Smith and I'll be more than happy to keep in touch with you. Thank you from the bottom of my heart Reuben. You're a saint. Are you this good to all your employees or do I get the special treatment? You've been good to me right from the day I started here. Where would I be without you?"

"You're a joy to know Angie, with your straight speaking and your energy. You're like a breath of fresh air wafting into a room. It's more than that though." His face suddenly looked unbearably sad. "The Nazis made sure I had no daughter when they took her, as a baby, with her mother. I like to think God sent you into my life to take her place. My second wife gave me three good sons but no daughter.

"That's horrendous. I'm so sorry you were a victim of their depravity. Perhaps it is God's work for us to be thrown together, especially after I lost Mum and Dad. Who knows? I'm not really into all that God stuff, but I can tell you, without any shadow of a doubt, I shall be eternally grateful that you're a part of my life.

Moving On

Angie spent a busy, lonely weekend compiling an information file for Lana as well as packing up all her personal belongings. She hired a car and a trailer, and by Monday midday she was ready to leave. She'd said an emotional 'goodbye' to Brian who had promised to tell all her neighbourhood friends that she'd left on family business.

She'd kept her telephone answering machine switched on for the entire weekend, just in case Rob telephoned with a redeeming explanation but there had been no contact from him. On the one hand that was deeply disappointing, while on the other, it made it easier for her to move on to pastures new. Exactly where that would be was as yet unknown; she'd know when she hit the right place.

With no particular destination in mind, Angie scanned her road map of America for inspiration. Where would she like to go? If she went north there was a possibility of extreme winter weather conditions and if she went south, she'd have to contend with the impossibly high temperatures and humidity of their summer. Heading west would probably be her best bet, making Chicago her first port of call. After all, she'd enjoyed city life in New York, so why not replace it with another big city? Decision made, Angie hit the highway; first stop Windy City.

Despite the surges of bleak emotion that periodically threatened to engulf her, Angie managed to get some pleasure out of her new adventure as she drove through what, for her, was new territory; it made her realize she'd never lost that joy of exploring she'd shared with her friends in her youth. Reaching the outskirts of Chicago she pulled off at a small motel, where, after driving all day, a warm shower, and a meal at the local diner, were more than welcome.

Next morning Angie again studied her road map, having decided after all that big city life wasn't what she wanted for her unborn child. Careful scrutiny showed her that Route 80 crossed the whole of the U.S.A., terminating in the west at San Francisco. Surely somewhere along its 2,900 miles she would find a place she could call home. She never dreamt that she'd travel the whole length of Route 80 before finding the right spot.

After Angie had been travelling for a week she telephoned Reuben as promised. "This is Esther Smith," she told the telephonist, trying to disguise her English accent. "Reuben is expecting my call." He was delighted to hear her voice.

"Where are you? Are you O.K.? I think about you every day, wondering where you are."

"I'm O.K. Reuben, how are you? I decided to head west and it's all going better than I'd hoped. I'm travelling Route 80 until I find somewhere I want to stop." When she told him about the places she'd stopped at along the way and the sights she'd seen, he was hugely relieved to hear a note of excitement in her voice.

"How's it going at the agency Reuben? Is Lana coping O.K?"

"Lana's doing swell. She got a new client just yesterday who's got her running around like a blue-tailed fly and she's loving every minute of it. Do you remember someone called Dolores Valanquez, one of New York's high-society ladies who does charity work in between shopping sprees? Well, she certainly remembers you and was all set for you to help her with a huge event she's planning. Apparently you made a big impression on her so she kept your card for when she might need you. She was disappointed to have missed you but she's decided to go with Lana. Thanks for the contact, Esther; this could be a big 'in' for us because if we can make her happy with this project her friends are sure to follow. Well done."

"Someone else was looking for you too; Rob. He called Ben Hudson to find out where you are but Ben could only tell him that you were away on family business. That's all Ben knows and that's all I know. What happens now is up to you."

"I miss him terribly but that was a long time for him to keep up a deception so I'll never be able to trust him again. I'll just carry on with my trip and ring you in a week's time. Perhaps I'll have found my new home by then. Fingers crossed! Bye for now Reuben. Talk to you soon."

Another ten days found Angie in San Francisco, still without any clear idea of where she wanted to live. She knew, almost instantly, that San Francisco was not the place for her, so she headed south towards Los Angeles in the hope that she might finally find somewhere suitable to unpack her belongings and take a rest from driving.

Some miles down the road, travel-weary and 'starving' Angie pulled off the highway and headed inland, aiming to stop at the first place that offered food. She didn't have to travel far before she hit Donny's Diner. Inside was bright and shiny, with a few locals sitting at the cheerful red tables in the little booths that lined the walls. A waitress, with 'Donny's Doughnuts' emblazoned across the chest of her scarlet top, approached Angie's table bearing a glass of iced water in one hand and her notepad in the other. "Hi hon, what can I get you today? Coffee to start?"

"I'd like a glass of milk and a chicken burger, thanks," replied Angie.

"Okay. Fries and salad come with it. I'm Rita. Just let me know if I can get you anything else." On her return with the milk and a huge plate of food, Rita cast an eye on the car park. "That your car and trailer? I can see it's not a number plate from round here; how far have you come?"

"New York."

"Wow, that's some journey. What brings you to this neck of the woods?"

"It's a long story that ends with me looking for somewhere to live. You've probably already guessed from the way I speak that I come from England. I'm completely on my own and what's more, until now, I've never been anywhere in America except for New York. I thought I might find somewhere to settle but it's so difficult. I'm not sure what I should do anymore. I can't travel forever. Or can I?"

Rita laughed, a deep, rasping, smoker's laugh. "Sounds to me like you've done enough travelling for now. What's your name hon?"

"Angie."

"Well, see here Angie, I ain't no expert on these things but it seems to me that you'll never know what a place is like if you don't stop there for a while. How d'ya know what makes a place tick if you ain't never spent any time there? This here's a neat little town; not too big and not too small. It's got a shopping mall, churches, library, cinema, sports area; you name it, we got'em all here in Paloma Bianca. We even got a real estate office down on the corner from here. Have your food, leave your car on our parking lot and go talk to Hank at the realtors. See what he has to say. Can't do no harm. You might find you want to give it a whirl for a short while; you can always move on when you're ready. Tell Hank Rita sent you."

That was some of the best advice Angie ever had. Hank was a man in his late forties, tall, tanned, bespectacled in a smart suit with shirt and tie. Chatting to him was so easy. He knew just the right questions to ask so that although Angie didn't know quite what she wanted when she walked into his office, when she walked out they'd established that she wanted a little house with a yard, in a respectable family-centred area near parks and good schools. He had three properties to show her right there in Paloma Bianca which he felt would suit her down to the ground.

Within a week Angie had settled into her new house, in a reasonable area with all the facilities she needed close to hand. When she next rang Reuben, he sighed a huge sigh of relief, happy to know that she was settled, at least for the present.

Starting Afresh

Angie loved her new home; it was exactly what she'd been looking for and she knew she was going to be very happy in that little house on Magdalena Street. During her first week 'in residence' she unpacked her belongings, visited the shopping mall several times, visited the library, found a doctor, a dentist and a paper boy, and met some of her new neighbours. She felt she'd fallen on her feet quite well.

The main tasks completed, the second week found her wondering what she should do with her time. She'd become so used to an office routine, it was difficult to fill all day every day without some kind of schedule. When the baby arrived it would be different but that was several months away. For the time being, she felt her lifestyle was aimless, a situation which couldn't be allowed to continue because it was completely foreign to her.

Her first small step in building a new life was to take herself off to the public library to borrow a book on the area, then walk to the nearby park with a packed lunch for a quiet read in the sunshine. There were always people around in the park and although they were all strangers, nevertheless, Angie enjoyed being amongst people and didn't feel quite so lonely.

Looking up from her book one day, she noticed a toy teddy bear lying forlornly on the path in front of her. There were no children in sight, except for a group over in the children's activity area, so Angie wandered over to see if she could find Ted's owner. As she approached she held the toy aloft. "Anyone lost this little guy?" she called. "He's kinda lonely." Immediately, a small raven-haired child of about four years old, came running towards her. "He's mine. He's my teddy. Where did you find him?" She took the toy from Angie, kissed him, then hugged him close to her chest.

Angie smiled. "He was lying on the path over by that bench." She pointed to where she'd been sitting. "He's so cute. I just knew someone must love him a lot."

A young woman, with hair similar to the little girl's, came wandering up. "Hi, there. Suzie was so eager to get to the swings, we didn't know Ted had gone missing. He's her best friend and it would break her heart if she ever lost him. Thank you so much for bringing him over. I'm Donna, and this is my daughter, Suzie. What do you say, Suzie?"

"Thank you so much. I do love him. What's your name?"

"Angie."

"I don't know anyone else called Angie. I've seen you sitting on that bench all by yourself reading your book. Have you got any children Angie?"

Donna took Suzie by the hand. "You ask a lot of questions Suzie. It's not always polite."

Angie didn't mind a bit. "No, I haven't any children. I'm on my own because I've just moved here and haven't any friends yet."

Donna was quick to respond. "In that case, come and sit with us and we'll introduce you to the others. We're all regulars here; I know they'd just love to meet you." Suzie took Angie's hand and dragged her across to a group of mothers with young children, saying, "This is Angie. She found Teddy. She's new. Mom says everyone has to say 'Hi' to her." From then on, Angie was never allowed to feel lonely in the park.

Most days, Angie got to the park early so that she could relax while she ate her lunch and read her book. Often, her solitude ended with the sound of running footsteps and the friendly cry of, "Hi Angie. I've brought Teddy to see you." Suzie usually gave Angie a big hug and then either plied her with quick-fire questions or grabbed her hand to drag her off to the swings. Angie found herself

103

drawn towards the friendly Donna, as well as finding the other women in the group easy company. She was enjoying her trips to the park.

One afternoon, Suzie arrived at the bench in quite a subdued mood. She stood in front of Angie, sucking her thumb, with Teddy dangling from her other hand. Donna was some way back along the path.

"Hi Suzie. No hug today? Are you O.K.?"

Suzie shook her head, quietly climbing up on the bench to sit next to Angie.

"Daddy's gone," she said.

"Gone where?"

"He's gone away. He shouted at Mommy, pushed her and then went away in the car. After that, two bad guys came round and they shouted at Mommy till they made her cry." Angie put her hand around the little girl, drawing her close.

Donna approached slowly, walking with a limp, carrying a large floral holdall. Angie noticed she was wearing large, white-framed sunglasses.

"Come and sit down for a while Donna. Sounds like you've got troubles."

"Yeah. There's no secrets when you've got kids." As she sat heavily on the bench, Suzie turned and clung to her. "What's Suzie told you?"

"She's told me her daddy's gone off in the car, with a few added details. I gather today's limp is all part of that."

Donna gave Suzie a big kiss. "Honey, would you like to go over and play with your friends while I have a little chat with Angie?" Suzie looked reluctant. "I'll be over soon. Don't worry; I'm not going anywhere. I promise. I just need a little rest. I'll wave to you when you get there."

Reassured, Suzie went off to play with her friends, periodically waving to her mother.

"What's it all about Donna? I know you were pushed over, but then Suzie said two rather unpleasant men came round. It sounds like a nightmare."

"It was no nightmare, Angie. It was the absolute truth, a situation that, I guess, I should have seen coming. I thought I knew it all, ignoring my family when they warned me not to marry Eddie; we were so in love but so very young. Despite that, everything worked out O.K. until Suzie was born, when I had to give up work to care for her. It meant that we didn't have much money so Eddie got involved in gambling; he was always going to win the big one. After he'd dug a hole so deep, he couldn't cope any more, he turned to drugs. I waited on tables in the evenings, while he looked after Suzie, and that gave me enough money to pay the rent. Just lately he's been so spaced out, I've been worried about leaving her with him but I didn't have any option; we needed the money.

Yesterday, when he came home from work, I knew there was something up. He dashed straight into the bedroom and started throwing things into a bag. When I asked what he was doing he just shouted angry stuff at me, telling me it was my fault for putting everything onto him, whatever that meant. Next, he started going through all my drawers and closets in a frenzy until he found where I'd hidden the rent money. I begged him to leave it but he just pushed me out of the way. That's when I fell awkwardly, twisting my leg. He tore out of the place like a madman, saying it was over between us, then drove off like a whirlwind, leaving me with no rent, no car and a twisted leg."

"I guess he also left you with a black eye behind those glasses."

Donna nodded bleakly.

"What's all this about two bad guys shouting at you?"

"It's what they shouted at me that's the big problem. It's all about Eddie's debts. They didn't believe he'd gone. They're going to keep checking to see if he's around and if they don't get their money they'll smash up the house. As if that weren't enough, they also said that if I don't tell them where he is, they'll harm me and Suzie." Donna's voice trailed away weakly as she began to tremble. "I've brought a few things out in this bag but I don't know where to go. If I go to church, the nuns might find us overnight shelter but they'll also get involved in the care of Suzie. I don't think I want to go down that route." She waved to Suzie on the swings, trying to put on a cheerful smile for her, without a great deal of success.

"You're both coming back to my place," said Angie firmly. "Is there anything else you need out of your house before they come back and wreck it?"

Shaking her head, Donna said, "I can't go back. I've never been so terrified in my life. Those guys mean business Angie."

"We'll see about that. I think we'd better go over to the others now before Suzie starts to panic."

Slowly, Angie walked beside Donna as she limped over to the happy group of mothers and children. As they approached, a tall, slim woman in blue jeans, with a colourful silky scarf tied round her head holding back her long, fair hair, loped across the remaining distance to put a comforting arm around Donna. "Hi, sweetie, don't tell me it's that excuse for a man again. I hope you got one in first." The three of them sat together on a bench. "It's getting too regular Donna. What's his beef this time? Whatever it is, it can't go on because you've got to stay strong for Suzie. She needs you."

"Same as usual Jacqui, except this time he's high-tailed it out of here, leaving me to deal with Sonny Bannerman's collectors. Two of his gorillas paid me a visit yesterday and threatened to return."

"No Donna. He's never gone and got you involved with Sonny Bannerman. That's real bad news. What are you going to do?"

"Good question, Jacqui. I wish I had the answer. Angie here's a star turn; she says we can stay with her tonight but I don't know what we're going to do after that. I don't seem to be able to get my head straight."

"Don't worry about tomorrow," soothed Angie. "Once we've got you over this hurdle you can sort out what happens next. There space at my place for the time being so that's no problem."

"You're the greatest Angie," said Jacqui, "a real friend in need." She looked at Donna's holdall. "Is that all you've managed to get out?"

"Yes. I couldn't carry anything without a car. I just grabbed what I could and got Suzie out of there before they came back."

Jacqui looked at Angie. "How much space have you got Angie? Can you cope with any of Donna's stuff if we can get it out safely?"

"Sure I can," replied Angie. "There's a whole garage standing empty. Feel free to fill it."

"But…" started Donna. "But nothing," interrupted Jacqui. "You need more than that bag, and what about Suzie's toys? What about her trike? She'll probably miss that more than she'll miss her daddy."

Jacqui beckoned some of the other mothers to give them a quick explanation of Donna's plight. Several had been in similar situations in the past and the general feeling was that Donna would be better off without the useless Eddy. Jacqui's idea was for a group of them to go to Donna's home to bring out as much as they could within a time limit of thirty minutes. They didn't want to court trouble by risking a meeting with Bannerman's stooges but they felt they should do something to help Donna avoid losing everything she had worked for over the past few years. Their demonstration of bravery and friendship gave Donna the courage to go with them to help decide what to take and what could be left behind. A couple of the women would care for the children in their mothers' absence, all except for Suzie. As she wouldn't be parted from her mother, it was decided she would sit outside in the car with Angie, who would keep an eye out for unwelcome visitors and warn the other women by blasting the horn.

It was a very tense half hour for all of them. They moved as swiftly as they could, constantly looking up and down the road for any sign of danger. Little Suzie sensed there was something in the air and asked Angie, "Will those bad guys be coming back?"

"No, Sweetie Pie," she lied, "and if they do, they won't find you because you'll be in my house, making sure I'm not lonely. Oh! Look Suzi! Jacqui's brought out your trike. You'll be able to ride that in my yard. We're going to have such fun."

Fortunately, the whole exercise went without a hitch and the group arrived at Angie's house with cars laden with Donna's most prized possessions. Their shrill laughter was edged with a tone of nervous relief as they set about stacking their booty in Angie's garage. Although they'd helped voluntarily, they were well aware of the risk they'd taken but they pushed those thoughts out of their minds, pleased and proud to have got one over on Sonny Bannerman and his merry men.

Finding One's Feet

Angie enjoyed having the company of Donna and Suzie; it brought a bit of vitality into her otherwise lonely home life. Suzie settled in like a duck to water but Donna had been badly affected by the incident. She felt safe in Angie's house but she daren't venture further than the back yard in case Bannerman's guys spotted her. She was in a constant state of anxiety, sleeping badly and losing weight. As trips to the park were out of the question, Angie issued an open invitation to their group of friends to call round any time. This worked quite well, resulting in a constant stream of visitors to Angie's little house on Magdalena Street.

Jacqui and her twin boys, Kurt and Scott, were frequent visitors. Angie got to know Jacqui quite well and commented one day, "How is it Jacqui that despite your hectic life you always manage to look so cool? Honestly, it doesn't matter what you do or what you wear. You'd even look good in a bin bag."

Her friend smiled. "You'd never think it now, but before the twins were born I was a model. I was happily married to an adoring husband who had a good income and I was here, there and everywhere on some pretty good photo shoots. I was all geared up for a screen test when I fell pregnant, so I had to let that opportunity go. I wouldn't change those kids of mine for anything, but, my oh my, did they make a difference to my life. Naturally, my work stopped but that didn't matter because Mike, my husband, was doing O.K. in his law firm. However, it only took six weeks for him to decide he couldn't live with kids, especially two of them. He took off with an actress he'd met while I was pregnant and we never set eyes on him again. He's good enough to send me a pittance to look after his sons while he lives the high life in Beverley Hills."

"Can't you get him for more maintenance?"

"My pride gets in the way; I'm not begging that man for anything. I've got a part-time job on the early shift at the fish processing plant. D'you know where I mean? It's the biggest employer in Paloma Bianca and if you can get in on the early shift, they pay higher rates than if you work more sociable hours."

"So what happens with Kurt and Scott while you're working?"

"I'm fortunate enough to be one of those people who have an insomniac for a mom." Jacqui laughed at the astonished look on Angie's face. "She sleeps in fits and starts for most of the night and as she doesn't live far away she's quite happy to come round to my place early so that I can get off to work. The boys tire her out and I suspect that probably enables her to manage a little sleep when she gets home. I appreciate what she does for me and I never ask any other favours from her."

"Will you go back to your modelling career when the boys are in school?" asked Angie.

Jacqui shrugged her shoulders. "Probably not. Apart from that being some time down the line, I also need a job that pays regularly when I'm raising the boys. Modelling pays better but it can also be erratic. It could work, but I guess I'm a little scared of thinking about going back. I feel as though the boys have taken over my whole life so that I don't exist anymore except as someone's Mom. How can I explain how it works so that you understand Angie? I rarely buy clothes any more, not only because I can't afford much but also because shopping with two active little children is a nightmare. It's impossible to try on a new pair of pants or a dress while I'm with them, so I do things to keep them happy instead."

"It must be very difficult," murmured Angie. "In fact, nigh on impossible. Don't you get fed up about it all?"

"Yeah, sometimes, then I look at their little faces... Coming here, or meeting the others at the park helps as most of us are in the same boat. We love our kids unconditionally but there's a heck of a price to pay."

Some of the women in the group were married and enjoyed a happy family life with a husband and one or more children. Many of the others had stories to tell similar to Jacqui's tale. They had literally been left holding the baby, whom they generally adored, but they felt completely tied down with money problems, work problems and caring problems that they felt took over their own lives and identities for twenty-four hours a day every day. The majority of them put their children's needs first, which meant their own needs were neglected. Careers were left behind as they took on any part-time job they could manage to organize around their children's needs. Paloma Bianca was an agreeable, small, residential town that didn't provide much in the way of jobs except for the fish processing plant, waiting on tables, bar work or pump attendant at either of the two local gas stations.

Meanwhile, Donna, sinking deeper and deeper into depression, felt she ought to make some effort to find work instead of being dependent on Angie. She knew the current situation couldn't continue but despite her daily good intentions, she couldn't muster enough energy to do much about it except read the 'Situations Vacant' column in the daily local paper; the lack of jobs on offer there made her feel even worse.

Donna's decline became increasingly obvious to her friends, until they decided they must do something to help. A few of them got together to discuss things as discretely as possible.

Mary Kay, mother of Ruby, a cute little girl about Suzie's age came up with an idea. "I went through hell when my guy did his disappearing act and I thought my world had come to end. I didn't eat or sleep and I didn't give a damn about how I looked. Well, Donna's got all that to cope with as well as worrying about those Bannerman bruisers. We've got to do something about giving her the confidence to walk out there again. Do you think we should help her create a disguise so that she can't be recognized?" The suggestion seemed to make sense to the group but they realized that achieving a credible disguise might be problematic, until Beth, a quiet, sensitive type, spoke up.

"I'd love to help out with this scheme. I'm still doing a bit of beautician work on a mobile basis. It's kind of difficult with Frankie here," she tousled her son's hair affectionately, "but I keep my hand in with a few clients. I could bring my stuff round and give Donna a completely new look. Let me talk to her, to tell her I want to do it as a present to cheer her up after all she's gone through lately." The idea met with everyone's approval, including Donna's, which was a great relief to the group. After Beth had worked her magic those present gathered round to see the results. The raven-haired Donna was now a dark, auburn-haired beauty with a smart, short hairstyle, reshaped eyebrows, subtle eye make-up, glossy lipstick and painted, manicured nails.

There was much oohing and aahing while they took in the transformation Beth had achieved. "Say, can you do anything with this?" asked big Sadie, as she ran her fingers through her dishevelled hair. They all laughed, as Sadie's appearance was never top of her priorities. "I know you won't be able to make me disappear, like you've done for Donna, but if you can do something with this bunch of feathers sprouting out of my head, I promise I'll brush it every single day." Sadie always knew how to raise a laugh.

Suzie had been at her mother's side during the whole process. "What do you think of Mommy today, Suzie?" asked Sadie. "Doesn't she look pretty?"

"My mom's beautiful and look what Beth's done for me. Do you think I look pretty too?" The little girl spread out her fingers and waved her tiny hands around proudly for everyone to admire her painted nails. There was no shortage of compliments from the onlookers.

Donna's new appearance gave her self-confidence a boost but she still broke out in a cold sweat whenever she attempted to walk anywhere. Thinking back to her youth, Angie came up with a possible solution to the problem. "Why don't you get yourself a dog Donna? There's always advertisements in the newspaper from people looking for good homes for unwanted pets. Let's take a look." Within a couple of days a large black and white dog of indeterminate parentage took up residence at Magdalena Street. Leo, as they named him, accompanied Donna everywhere and at last she summoned up the courage to venture away from home, much to the delight of her daughter and her friends.

The next task facing Donna was to give some serious attention to finding work. She looked at the newspaper every day, rang possible employers in the telephone directory and even called into places around the centre of Paloma Bianca but all without success. She tried hard but it was difficult not to become dispirited.

"Why are you contacting all these places directly?" asked Angie. "Wouldn't it be easier to sign on with a recruitment agency? If you need help with their fee, I'll lend you the money and you can repay me when you're working."

"What recruitment agency? This is Paloma Bianca, not L.A. Another thing is, I need to work locally to be near Suzie, which raises an additional problem. I shall have to find a babyminder with reasonable rates so that means I shall probably be best finding evening work because then I might find a teenager who'll do it cheaply. They often like to make a few dollars while they do their homework."

"It certainly isn't easy," said Angie thoughtfully. "It seems to me that there must be a lot of people chasing the few jobs Paloma Bianca is able to offer. Not everyone is going to be lucky."

"I'll just have to keep trying; you never know what might turn up," said her friend optimistically.

The Idea

Watching her friend go through the soul-destroying process of the daily search for work, disturbed and frustrated Angie. Never one to sit around feeling helpless, she came up with an idea. Initially, it was only the germ of an idea but then the more she thought about it the bigger it grew, until she became so excited about it, she rang her old friend Reuben back in New York.

"Hello, this is Esther Smith. Would you put me through to Reuben please?""

"Hi Angie. How are things with you?"

"Great. I hope everything's O.K. with you too." Rushing on, she said, "Reuben, I have an idea I want to run past you, if you have the time."

"You're in luck Angie. What's the idea?"

"I want to open a recruitment agency here in Paloma Bianca with a day nursery attached for the use of the clients. I've done some research, I've pinpointed suitable premises and I've even created a business plan. I'm serious about this."

"I don't doubt you're serious, Angie. What brought all this on? Tell me more."

Angie told him how she'd spoken to a lot of people in the area, particularly the women. Many of them would like to work, or need to work, but there were problems. The main problem was finding affordable childcare. Once that was available the jobseekers could then be persuaded to look for work further afield than Paloma Bianca. That was where she, Angie, could step in with her experience at the Burlington Recruitment Agency back in the U.K. as well as a certain amount of involvement she'd had with Reuben's recruitment department at the marketing agency.

Reuben listened very carefully. "I've got my business cap on now Angie. I know you'll be able to find clients looking for work but how do you plan to find your clients looking for workers?"

"I've already identified some targets. I've also costed out a mailshot campaign which I'll follow up on the telephone. I have every confidence I can do it."

"Who am I to query your confidence? You've never lacked in that department. Next question is, how do you intend financing this project?"

"That's why I'm ringing you Reuben. I want to approach a bank but I wanted to talk to you first to find out what you think about the idea. Do you think it's feasible?"

"First impressions are pretty good, but I would need to see your plan, costings, etc. to give you a considered opinion. Meanwhile, I have another question. When do you intend putting your plan into action, seeing as how you are now, how many months pregnant?"

"Good point. The answer is, as soon as possible. The fact is, I've time on my hands at the moment to get everything up and running smoothly. Once the baby is here it won't be so easy to do a business start-up."

"O.K. Angie. I have to be honest and tell you that I was looking for ways of extending the business here. If your plan stands up to scrutiny, I'll put some money in for you. I'm cheaper than the banks. We could come to some arrangement about repayment. Send me the paperwork and I'll have a look at it."

"You're the greatest, Reuben. Would you be surprised to know that I've already mailed a big fat envelope to you with all the information you'll need? One other thing, I've decided on a name for the agency; it's going to be Smart Choice."

Two weeks later, Angie had leased her building of choice via her contact with Hank at the real estate office

116

and had engaged a team of builders to make the appropriate alterations for a day nursery centre on the ground floor and offices for the recruitment agency on the next floor. The workmen were well aware that she needed the work to be completed as quickly as possible but they hadn't expected her to make a daily visit to inspect progress.

Meanwhile, Angie was working from home in an effort to hit the ground running just as soon as the building was ready for occupation. She sent out her mailshot to part of the greater Los Angeles area as well as her local area. That was followed up with long hours on the telephone persuading prospective employers why they should use her recruitment agency for their personnel requirements. She had the expected overall mixed response but was overjoyed with the number of positive responses she achieved. One of her main sectors of attention was the numerous movie studios in the area which she saw as a huge potential source of employment. She discussed with them their requirements for cleaners, porters, drivers, clerical staff, caterers, etc., etc., as well as their constant need for movie extras. Meticulous notes were made on every call she made. Any contact names and numbers were carefully recorded for future use. Good progress was made but Angie knew there was no place for complacency and kept at it, day after day.

Donna, too, made valiant efforts to help get the new project up and running. Every day she set out, with Suzie and Leo in tow, to deliver flyers to potential clients in Paloma Bianca. Rita, at Donny's Donuts was very enthusiastic. "This is just what Paloma needs. I'll see that one of these is served with every order. Best of luck hon." Shoppers at the mall were handed flyers, people in the parks, parents outside school gates, as well as the many cafés, restaurants and bars in the town. By the time the building was ready for use, the word had been spread to most of Paloma Bianca.

When the opening day arrived there were three members of staff to greet clients. Angie would deal with employment enquiries and enrolments. Marie, a qualified nursery worker had been employed to run the day nursery, and Donna would go between the two, helping wherever she could to keep things running smoothly. Suzie, along with her cuddly Ted, was the first member of the nursery.

Angie opened the door with a mixture of both excitement and trepidation, although she needn't have worried because the venture got off to a rousing start. Enrolment for workers was free, while employers paid a fee for every employee the agency provided. Several of the mothers from the park enrolled, Jacqui being one of the first to walk through the door.

"What kind of work are you looking for?" asked Angie. "Are you thinking of going back to modelling if the twins are in the day nursery? Did you know that if you find work through our agency we charge only a minimum fee for their care? Donna will give you the information."

"I don't think I could make the grade in modelling anymore; I have to face the fact that they're looking for younger girls. However, I thought I might get some work in promotions. I could see myself doing that kind of thing."

"Have you ever thought of auditioning as a movie extra? I'm working hard on getting some of those jobs for the agency. Would you like to go on the list? We'll also look for other work for you." A delighted Jacqui floated out of the door with high hopes of actually being able to quit her job at the fish processing plant.

Big Sadie also turned up to "check out the joint." She needed work but had no training for anything in particular. She didn't want bar work but would try her hand at whatever else turned up. Also, she had wheels and was prepared to travel out of Paloma Bianca. Angie felt sure they could find something for her, especially if she was prepared to go on their temp. list for cleaners, carers, shoppers, dog walkers, etc. Sadie was so pleased, she promised to send in her niece to see if they could do anything to help her. "She's a good kid at heart but she's been mixing with some bad company. I've promised my sister I'll help get her straightened out."

As soon as the girl walked through the door next day, Angie guessed it must be Sadie's niece. She was wearing tight, white trousers with a cropped, powder blue, off the shoulder top. Her dull, lifeless hair, wisped around her prematurely careworn face while the heavy eye make-up and pale lipstick did nothing to enhance her looks. A tall girl, she teetered across the floor in high, strappy red sandals. "Hi. I'm Debbie," she said. "Big Sadie sent me over here to talk to you." She sat in the chair, opposite Angie, and blew an enormous bubble, then continued chewing, occasionally burping quietly.

Angie took some information then finally told Debbie, "I'm sorry Debbie but I have to tell you, in my present state," she patted her large bump, "I can't stand the smell of that gum you're chewing. Do you mind getting rid of it?"

Debbie looked like a startled rabbit. "I'm so sorry. I didn't mean to upset you." She swiftly took the offending pink blob from her mouth and was about to dispose of it when Angie intervened. "No Debbie, not there. Please don't stick it under the table." A look of amazement spread across the girl's face. Angie handed her a tissue. "Wrap it in this and drop it in the bin." Debbie gave her an incredulous look, shrugged her shoulders slightly and did as she was bid.

"Would you like to tell me something about yourself Debbie so that I can get an idea of how we can help you? What kind of work have you done in the past?"

"There ain't much to tell. I didn't like school so I hightailed it out of there just as soon as I could and joined a group I'd been singing with for a while. We thought we were going to hit the big time but it never happened; all they hit was the drugs scene. It took me a while to realize that it wasn't for me but I didn't want to crawl home with my tail between my legs saying, "You were right Mom. I got it all wrong." She cocked her head on one side and gave Angie a rueful grin.

Continuing, she said, "I tried various jobs but the problem was, I hadn't trained for nothin'. I could sing but a lot of girls could sing better than me. In the end, I finished up working mostly in bars. The last job I had was at a bar in Bakersfield. Most of the guys who came in thought they were twenty years younger and twenty pounds lighter than they really were. A few drinks inside them and they thought they were every girl's dream of Mr. Heartthrob. I could deal with their corny chat-up lines as long as there was a bar between them and me; they were harmless enough. What I didn't like was when Joe, the new barman, was set on and he started to get fresh with me. If I'd complained to the boss, Joe would have denied it and I would probably have been fired as there were plenty of girls willing to take my place. When talking to him, or even yelling bad names at him, had no effect, I decided I wouldn't take it any longer. Next time he stood behind me, rubbing up close to me, I kept my cool and slowly twisted round to face him wearing a big 'come and get it' smile. He thought it was his lucky day, especially when I started to undo his jeans. As he lunged forwards to kiss me, ugh, I plunged my hand into the ice bucket and dropped a good big handful of ice down his pants. He moved quicker than a scalded cat, yelling every foul word his momma never taught him. I wish you could have seen his face." Both Angie and Debbie laughed at the picture she'd just painted. "That was when I quit and returned to Paloma Bianca to do, I don't know what. Have you got any idea about what I should do?"

Angie leaned back in her chair, looking thoughtful. "Sorry to ask this, but have you got any criminal record because I might have to make checks if you take up an idea I have for you."

"No. I might have lived on the edge but I know right from wrong."

"Good, because I like you Debbie and I think we could get along together so I'm going to give you a chance. It's not long until my baby's due and I'll have to take a week or so away from work. Donna will run the agency in my absence but that means we'll need to fill her empty post on a temporary basis. Because she helps out in both the recruitment office and the day nursery, it would give you quite a wide job experience. Would you fancy working with her to learn her job so that you're ready when the baby decides to make an entrance?"

"Wow! I ain't never done nothin' like this before. Do you really think I could do it?"

"I wouldn't offer you the job if I didn't. It's up to you whether or not you choose to give it a go. If you decide on yes, we'll talk hours, money and presentation."

"I understand the hours and money but what do you mean by presentation? Do I have to make a presentation? I'm not too sure about that part."

"Let me explain. This is a new company, a company I'll do everything in my power to make a success. That's why we have to be absolutely professional in everything we do. The way we work, the way we treat people and the way we look. Now, you're a very attractive girl but you don't look professional. I'm waiting for a delivery of customised tops to arrive. They'll be black with our company logo in red and gold on the shoulder. Will you be prepared to wear one with either red or black pants? Also, you'll need more subtle make-up and your hair either shorter or tied back. Do you get the picture of what I'm aiming at?"

"You sure know what you want. I ain't never been asked to dress like that before but if you're willing to give me a chance, then it's not too much to ask in return. I'll do it. I'm scared but I'll do my best."

Angie held out her hand. "Welcome on board Debbie. I'm truly glad you're going to join us. You'll find I'm quite strict in some ways but, at the same time, if you need any help or you have any ideas of your own, I'm always prepared to listen. Let me introduce you to Donna."

Debbie took to her new job as though she were born to it. The children in the day nursery adored her, following her everywhere, and in return, she thrived on their love and trust. She tried hard in the recruitment side of the agency but it didn't take her long to decide that eventually she'd like a permanent job in the nursery. She was surprised by her choice of career, as was her Aunt Sadie and the rest of the family. No one had guessed that Debbie had that something special it takes to work with small children.

After a very busy couple of weeks at the agency, Debbie went up to Angie's office to ask if there were any possibility of staying on permanently in the day nursery after Angie's return from maternity leave.

"I'm glad you came to see me," said Angie. "I've had excellent comments from both staff and parents about your work in the nursery. I think you've found your niche Debbie. As it happens, the whole project has taken off even better than I'd ever hoped for and we'll definitely need more staff in order to cope with the workload. I've discussed nursery staffing with Marie and she suggested that I might ask you to stay on as you're doing so well and there's a need for another full-time worker to handle the daily increase in the number of children placed with us."

Pleased and proud, Debbie returned to her charges feeling this was the best thing that had ever happened to her. Determined always to do her best for Angie, she became one of the agency's most long-serving members of staff.

Big Sadie and her sister were delighted by the outcome, happy that at last Debbie was finally settled. However, Sadie not only had cause to be pleased about her niece, but also on her own account. Smart Choice had no problem in finding part-time domestic work in the Los Angeles area for Sadie and several other clients but not all of those enrolled had transport to travel to out-of-town jobs. In order to satisfy the demand for jobs and workers, Angie asked Big Sadie if it were possible for her to give one or two of the women a lift in her car in return for a small contribution towards her motoring costs. The plan went ahead to everyone's satisfaction and very soon Sadie saw her opportunity. After discussing her idea with Angie, she bought a larger vehicle and set up in business as Sadie's Transport, working closely with Smart Choice to plan transport schedules for taking staff to and from work for very reasonable charges. Other work soon came her way, especially from groups of senior citizens who were no longer able to drive to the shopping mall, day centres, social outings etc. The friendly figure of Big Sadie and her transport quickly became well known around town, satisfying a need for many of Paloma Bianca's residents.

By the time Angie's baby arrived, she was satisfied with the progress made at Smart Choice and felt able to turn her attention to motherhood in the knowledge that her business was in safe hands.

Family Life

"Hello, this is Esther Smith. Would you put me through to Reuben, please?"

"Hi, Angie. How's the world with you?"

"It's a boy Reuben. A beautiful baby boy. He's just two hours old and I wanted you to be one of the first to know. I can't believe he's real. It's like a miracle just happened. If I had any energy left I'd be dancing round the room for pure joy."

"I'm delighted for you Angie. Let me wish you both good health and happiness. May you enjoy all the gifts motherhood will surely bring you."

"Thank you so much. Do you want to know what I've called him? He's Robert Edward Reuben Caswell, after the three most important men in my life. What d'you think of that?"

Reuben gave a happy chuckle. "That's quite a name for such a little guy to carry. I can't believe you called him Reuben, Angie. That's very moving. Thank you."

"Well, if I'm your surrogate daughter, I decided you should be a surrogate grandfather so I gave him your name. You're right, it is a grand name for my little cutie but that's his formal name. Generally, he'll be known as Rusty; there's already signs that his hair's going to be the same colour as his father's. Speaking of whom, do you ever see him around?"

"Come to think of it, I've only seen him about twice since you left and that was in the early days. I haven't seen him recently but then, I wouldn't expect him to visit us quite so often. We still hold their account but that's running smoothly after the initial flurry of work and I think another Brit comes over occasionally when necessary. Are you thinking of getting in touch with him about little Rusty?"

"No. I've given it a lot of thought and decided to let sleeping dogs lie. We were both truly, madly in love with each other but it seems our affair was on a false footing and doomed to collapse. It was a wonderful time in my life, one I don't think I'll ever be able to repeat with such intensity and I'm grateful I knew true love; nothing can take away my wonderful memories. Now, I have to move on with this new little man in my life. I'll send you some photographs. I might even come up to New York to introduce you to him before he's much older."

"Just say the word. I look forward to seeing you again and meeting my namesake. Take care, Angie and don't go rushing back to work too quickly. I don't know why I said that because I know you'll do it your way as usual. However, do take care."

Reuben was right. Angie was back at Smart Choice within a couple of weeks, proudly carrying Rusty into her office in his Moses basket. Fortunately, he was a happy, placid child always wreathed in smiles and so there was always willing help to care for him.

At home, Donna stayed on partly to help Angie through the first stages of motherhood and partly to enable her to save enough funds to get a home and transport so that she and Suzie could start anew. Suzie was in no rush to leave behind her new 'brother' as she called him. It was a very happy home for the four of them, one that no one was hurrying to change.

Three years later, Donna and Suzie were still part of the household in Magdalena Street. Word had filtered through on the grapevine some time earlier that Sonny Bannerman had eventually cornered Eddie, Donna's errant ex-husband. Apparently he now worked as a bag man for Bannerman and was known as Eddie the Gimp. He never tried to renew his ties with Donna, who was greatly relieved as it enabled her to carry on with her life with renewed confidence, safe in the knowledge that the menace that was Bannerman would no longer jump out of the shadows demanding information on her ex.

One evening, Angie and Donna were relaxing after having got the children to bed when Donna said, "I enrolled a real nice guy today called Bill Bassett, a plumber by trade, who's having a hard time since his wife died of cancer and left him to bring up their daughter all on his own. He decided he'd go onto our temp. list and will take any type of work for the time being. His little girl, Belle, a real cutie, starts at the day nursery tomorrow and I've found him some work as a gardener out in The Hills. He says he needs to be sure Belle has settled in O.K. at the nursery before he looks for a full-time day job. He's been doing bar work in the evenings while a neighbour's daughter babysits. I think he must be our first male single parent."

"Interesting," said Angie, hugging her mug of coffee. "I'll let you know if we get hold of any plumbing jobs."

A couple of months later, the two women were again enjoying their evening cup of coffee, after the rigours of bedtime for the children, when once more Donna brought up the subject of Bill Bassett.

"I caught up with Bill Bassett today when he was collecting Belle. He loves the job you found him with Taylors. He's so glad to go out to work again knowing that Belle is thriving at the Day Nursery. What a nice guy."

"Yeah, you tell me that every time you mention his name."

Donna's complexion was slightly tinged with pink, as she continued. "Actually, I have a favour to ask you. Bill wants to cook me a meal to celebrate him getting things back on an even keel and feeling like a normal person again. Would you mind keeping an eye on Suzie for me tomorrow evening while I go over to his place? Suzie will be in bed by the time I leave."

"No problem. I had a teeny weeny suspicion something was brewing between the pair of you. Have a nice evening."

Six months later the two friends were again discussing Bill Bassett. Donna was talking very earnestly. "Are you sure you'll be O.K.? After all you've done for me, I don't want you to feel I'm leaving you in the lurch. You just have to say the word and I'll tell Bill we'll have to carry on as we are now because I can't desert you and Rusty."

Angie shook her head emphatically. "Stop worrying. We both knew our arrangement wouldn't last forever. We've got on like a house on fire and I'm too fond of you to spoil your chance of happiness with Bill. I like Bill; you're meant for each other, so go ahead, grab this chance with both hands and make it work. Be happy." She threw her arms around Donna in a tight hug.

Next day, Rusty came crying to his mother. "Suzie's going to live with her new daddy," he wept. Angie picked him up onto her lap. "Don't cry sweetie, we'll still see her and Auntie Donna. You'll see."

"Yes," he wailed, "but why can't I have a daddy?"

"You already have a daddy," explained his mom, "who lives far across the sea. He loves us but he's very busy and it's difficult for him to come and see us. Perhaps Suzie will share her daddy with you." Suzie came running across the room to hug Rusty. "Don't be sad Rusty. You already know my new daddy; it's Bill. I don't mind sharing him. Come and play." That was the first of surprisingly few questions about Rusty's father over the following years, all of which Angie managed to answer with a conciliatory version of the truth but without ever resorting to lies.

The years sped by with Angie happily juggling her career and her role as doting mother to her popular son. They were good years, with the house in Magdalena Street teeming with life and laughter as it offered 'open door' hospitality to both Rusty's and Angie's friends and neighbours. They were such absorbing, busy years that it came as a bit of shock to find time had crept up on them and Rusty was looking forward to graduating from high school. Decisions were made about his future and it was a proud but sad Angie who waved him off on his journey to university.

The house was a very quiet place without her beloved son. Occasional visits from friends were no substitute for the lively vitality of having him around. Ever practical, Angie searched for a solution and made the decision to move on from Magdalena Street, recognizing it would never be the same again. When she rang Rusty to tell him she was thinking of moving into a new luxury apartment block which had just been built in Paloma, he said, "Go for it Mom. Sounds like a great idea. Just remember to give me the address when you've moved so that I don't turn up at Magdalena by mistake."

He was right; it was a good idea. Angie had just adapted to her new way of life when the intriguing letter arrived like a bolt out of the blue and here she was, again with his encouragement, on a plane bound for the U.K. to follow up a mysterious invitation from a firm of solicitors unknown to her until now.

Return of the Native

As Angie entered the arrivals hall at Heathrow Airport she scoured the crowd and was rewarded by the sight of her name on a display board being held aloft by a man in a smart chauffeur's uniform. Courteously, he took her case and escorted her to a sleek, black car to whisk her through the chaotic streets of London to a smart office block in Mayfair, where she was swiftly taken up to the office of, Mr. Giles Hobson, a senior partner in the firm of Stephens, Hobson and Wilson.

He introduced himself, adding, "I hope you had a good flight Miss Caswell. May I offer you some tea? It's always refreshing after a long trip."

"That would be very welcome. I've been looking forward to a cup of good old British tea. Thank you."

After the pleasantries, Mr. Hobson got down to business. "You must be wondering what this is all about but our client was very specific and we have a duty to follow his instructions to the letter. Now, I'm sorry to trouble you but may I see the identification documents we requested?"

Having checked the documents, the solicitor continued. "As solicitors to the late Mr. Robert Anderson..." Angie gasped. "The late Robert Anderson. You mean ...?" She gripped the arms of her chair, her knuckles gleaming white, as the room began to spin. From somewhere far, far away, she heard a faint, anxious voice saying, "Are you alright Miss Caswell? Would you like a glass of water?" Speechless, she shook her head; this was the last thing in the world she'd expected.

"I'm so sorry you've learned of Mr. Anderson's demise in this way. It must be a terrible shock for you. Are you able to continue or would you like time to recover?"

"Thank you for your concern. It's many years since I was last in touch with Mr. Anderson and this has indeed come as a dreadful shock. However, I think we'd better continue."

"First of all I need to pass on to you this letter and this small package. I have no knowledge of their contents; they are explicitly for your eyes only. I shall now go on to inform you of the contents of the will. Lord Arnechester, also known as Mr. Robert Benedict Anderson, has bequeathed his entire estate to you, Miss Angela Marjorie Caswell. The majority of his estate is in the form of some quite considerable financial investments which will be explained to you by a representative of his bank who will discuss them with you shortly. In addition, he has nominated you as the sole heir, or should I say heiress, to the house and land known as the Larchridge Estate in North Yorkshire. The entire contents of the house are also yours, Miss Caswell. I'm sure you must have some questions and I shall be happy to help you in any way I'm able."

Angie was stunned and after a heavy session with the bank manager, she felt her brain had reached absolute saturation point. Robert had been fabulously rich and had left everything to her. In a daze, she was escorted to her nearby hotel where, once in the privacy of her own apartment, she poured herself a stiff drink and opened the parcel Rob had insisted should be given to her.

Reaching carefully into the package, Angie brought out a small ring box covered in soft, scarlet leather. The lid of the box opened to reveal an exquisite ring of tiny overlapping, alternate gold and platinum hearts. The inscription inside the ring read, "Forever." When Angie slipped the ring on her finger it was a perfect fit, and that was when she reached her breaking point. The brave face she'd put on suddenly crumpled as she broke down and sobbed uncontrollably, weeping floods of scalding, heartrending tears; tears which had been stored away too many long years.

Later, having lain motionless on the sofa, without any sense of time, watching the evening sun go down, she eventually summoned up the energy to open the letter that had accompanied the ring package. It read as follows.

My Darling Angie,

First, let me apologise for the mystery, but I thought that if you saw my name you might refuse the invitation I'd asked my solicitors to send you.

I have so many things to tell you and I think it would be best if I started where we left off, on what was going to be a very special evening for both of us, until the dreaded telephone call. I think you know by now that it was my wife, not my mother, at the other end of the line. She'd decided to visit me on the spur of the moment, for the first time ever. I'm sorry I lied to you, but you see, I had planned to tell you the whole truth about my situation that very evening. I was too cowardly to tell you earlier because I was terrified I might lose you.

My plan for our special evening was to give you the ring I'd designed and had made for you; I'd gone to get it when the telephone rang. I was going to explain that I was married and intended to ask my wife for a divorce. I was going to beg your forgiveness for my deceit and ask you to marry me.

The telephone call completely scuppered my wonderful plans. I knew I would have to approach the situation very carefully with my wife as we are both Roman Catholics and divorce is a delicate issue. If she'd met you before I'd discussed it with her, she'd have blown her top and I wouldn't have stood a chance, not that it made much difference because she hit the roof anyway and stubbornly refused to listen any further that evening.

Next day I suggested we take a break up-state, partly so that we might be able to discuss things more calmly and partly because I couldn't bear her being so disagreeable in what was our apartment, the home you and I had created together.

We stayed away for almost a week but I couldn't persuade her to even consider a divorce; she said our vows were forever and wouldn't recognize that mistakes can be made or that situations can change. I was living on a knife edge during those few days, desperately trying to get her to see reason, and so I'm sorry, my darling, but I daren't get in touch with you in case she discovered me and flipped altogether. When I finally returned home, you'd flown the nest and no one could tell me where you were. I guessed you'd found out the truth about my situation.

I tried to find you but it was shortly afterwards that I became ill. I was flown home by private jet in the care of my own U.K. doctors and after weeks of recovery, tests, etc. they diagnosed multiple sclerosis. I eventually made a reasonably good recovery from that first bout, enabling me at last to appoint a firm of investigators to try to find you because I wanted to let you know that my unpredictable wife had had second thoughts and had decided to agree to a divorce. Despite their best efforts, it was a few years before my people discovered where you were living and by that time you seemed quite happily established in your new life and, unfortunately, my illness had progressed.

I experienced periods of remission with MS but each time I was ill, it took its dreadful toll until I could no longer walk. At that point I gave up my business activity and retired to my home in North Yorkshire. I still had the use of my hands and most of my other faculties and so I took the opportunity to return to my artwork while I was still able. At least my painting gave me some sense of purpose and a certain amount of satisfaction. By that time I was resigned to the fact that this cruel disease is relentless and that I would continue to decline, with fewer periods of remission.

When my investigators provided me with photographs of you and your son, I longed to see you both. I guessed that our suspicions were confirmed and that he is our son, with your curls and my colouring. How I wish I'd known him; I hope he doesn't think too badly of me. After long days and nights of dithering, I finally decided not to intrude on your happiness. You are so full of life and energy, my darling, I couldn't think of inflicting my burden on you. Even if you'd had me back, nothing would have been the same. I couldn't ask you to make that sacrifice. You should have your chance to live life to the full.

There hasn't been a day when I haven't thought of you and the love and light you brought into my life. You are wonderful and the time we spent together was perfect. We knew true love, you and I, even though it was for a relatively short time. Some people live a long life and never experience what you and I shared. Thank you, a million times over. I shall love you forever.

There are other things that I should explain to you, like why, in some official papers, am I referred to as Lord Arnechester? That is because I am the only heir of my father, the late Lord Arnechester. My family lived in the border counties for generations but when my grandfather died they were hit hard by death duties and sold off most of their estates. My parents moved to Larchridge in North Yorkshire to start anew, the property there being the only one they had managed to retain. They believed the title was worth very little without the ancestral home and decided that I should take my mother's family name. So, I have a name as well as a title. I'm telling you this because I think both you and our son should know something about my background.

I've lived in relative seclusion at Larchridge over my last few years but I haven't been lonely. I have my memories, especially of you, I have a few close friends and I couldn't have had a better staff to care for me. I've *also been fortunate enough to afford every comfort anyone could desire.*

When father was alive he was involved in the farm at Larchridge, but I've had no interest in those matters and so you will find much of the land is leased to local farmers even though it will be in your ownership.

The house has always had a special draw for me and my earnest hope is that you might feel the same about it. If not, then feel free to do with it as you will. I leave you everything I own to enable you to live life to the full, whatever that means to you. Live for both of us, my darling. Be carefree. Be fulfilled. Be happy.

Don't mourn my final departure Angie. I've done my best, with the help of others, to keep in good spirits but I'm starting to feel I've endured this failing body long enough and when my end comes it will be a welcome relief. Take my ring and believe that my love for you is forever, our hearts will always remain entwined. Nothing can change that, so go forward and meet what life has to offer and should you meet love again, welcome it with open arms and let it into your life. No one can have too much love.

One last thing; believe me when I say that everything I did and every decision I made was motivated by the best of intentions. If I have hurt you or made you sad, please forgive me. I wouldn't intentionally harm a hair on your head. With your forgiveness I know I shall rest in peace.

I have one deep regret in life and that is not knowing my son. I received photographs and reports from my people and felt satisfied he thrived in your care and has grown into a young man who would make any parent proud. I have loved him from afar and wish him well in life. I ask his forgiveness and understanding.

I can't bring myself to say those final words, my angel; perhaps it's because there still hovers a tiny, golden ray

*of hope that a small fragment of me will remain forever
in your heart.*

Forever yours,   Rob

Angie read, then re-read, those precious words until
eventually, exhausted, she sank into a deep, dreamless
sleep, the letter still clutched in her hand.

Facing the Future

Next morning, Angie slept later than usual, gradually awaking from her slumbers aware of a sense of anxiety hanging heavily upon her consciousness. As she moved, a rustle of paper reminded her of the letter and the bizarre events of the previous day, launching her back into the reality of her situation. After ordering coffee and croissants from room service, she remained in the comfort of her luxurious surroundings to study further Rob's letter and the wad of paperwork she'd received from the solicitors and the bank. A constant stream of questions flooded her mind. Had she been too hasty? Had she been too judgemental? Should she have contacted Rob after Rusty was born? Had she spoiled everything for all three of them?

After several cups of coffee and a lot of deep thought, Angie came to the conclusion that it was pointless trying to hypothesize about the past. What's done is done. She had decided she could never trust him again based on what she knew then, not on what she had only recently learned. Also, Rob wanted her to remember him as he was, not as an invalid, dependent upon her or others. Sadly, rationale couldn't quite conquer the emotional turmoil she was suffering nor the torrents of tears. However, there was one redeeming feature from which she gained great consolation. The two of them were as one in remembering their time together as something special, something unique, the memory of which nothing could ever erase. They had known true love for each other and that would last forever. She fingered the ring as though to confirm the irrefutable truth.

After a morning of pondering, questioning and weeping, the practical Angie kicked in, urging her to get out of bed, take a shower, then decide what her next course of action should be. Refreshed, she set about making arrangements to visit Larchridge. After all, that was where Rob had spent his last years and perhaps she could reconnect with him somehow by just being in the place that he'd loved, where he'd found some comfort. Arrangements were made for her to meet Mr. and Mrs. Pringle, the general caretakers of the property, at 2 p.m. next day. They'd be pleased to show her around and answer any queries she may have.

So it was that Angie set out in her hired car, with a tingle of excitement replacing the tears of the previous two days. Always one for adventure, she looked forward to exploring somewhere new, especially as it was a place that Rob had obviously known well. Driving north up the M1 motorway, to her surprise, she experienced an unexpectedly sharp pang of homesickness when she saw the signs which would take her back to Millbeck. It was such a long time since she'd visited. Would it still be the same, quaint, old-fashioned village she'd known as a child? Would she still know any of the people there? Pushing all such thoughts to the back of her mind, she continued on her way to North Yorkshire, focussing on the road that would lead her to Larchridge.

Turning off the long, tedious motorway, she drove through small, rural towns and villages until, at last, she was out on the open road, hills and dales to either side, with ribbons of grey, dry-stone walling stretching as far as the eye could see. Now she could understand why Yorkshiremen proudly called it 'God's own country'. Driving at a leisurely pace, Angie followed the instructions she'd been given by the solicitors and looked for a sign on the right-hand side, after a bridge and a sharp bend in the road.

There it was; a sign directing her to Larchridge. It took her up a narrow lane, bound on both sides by stone walls fronted by a tangle of fern and flowers and the occasional clump of trees, mainly larch. The road widened slightly when it came to a small hamlet of about six houses and a farm. Continuing, she came to a gravel drive with a huge wooden gate, propped wide open, bearing the sign

Larchridge. The drive, lined by beautiful larch trees with their wispy fronds swaying in the breeze, wound uphill, round to the left and finally revealed a magnificent, large stone house standing proudly in the bright sunshine against a backdrop of hills dotted with tiny white sheep in the distance.

This couldn't possibly be her house. There must be some mistake. Perhaps if she made enquiries they would direct her to the house where Rob had spent his last days. She scrunched across the gravel and tugged on the bell-pull to the side of the expansive oak door, enjoying the view as she waited until she heard the sound of footsteps approaching from the other side of the door. A grey-haired woman with a ruddy complexion, wearing sensible trousers and a beige, woollen sweater, opened the door, to greet Angie with a friendly smile. Before Angie could speak, the woman said, "You'll be Miss Caswell. We've been expecting you." Opening the door wider, she continued, "Do come in and I'll have you a cup of tea made in next to no time. I hope you had a good journey up here." Quickly adjusting to the situation, Angie entered to find herself in a large, oak-panelled hall hung with portraits and landscapes. A huge pair of deer antlers was mounted over a door at the rear. Ushering Angie into a cosy room off to the left, where a glowing log fire burned in the grate, the woman told her, "I'm Mrs. Pringle. I've worked here at the house for most of my life and I served Mr. Anderson till the end. My husband, Jim, and I have always looked after the house for him and have quarters on the second floor. Jim also used to do a bit of gardening but his back's not so good these days and so he gets a younger fellow in to give him a hand. I'll be back in a minute or two with that cup of tea.

True to her word, she soon returned bearing a gleaming silver tray laden with scones, cakes and tiny sandwiches, as well as a large silver teapot and everything else that was needed for a good cup of tea.

"I'm going to leave you now so that you can enjoy your tea in peace and have a bit of a rest if you fancy it, especially after that long drive. Just press that bell at the side of the fireplace when you're ready for me to show you around." Off she bustled, reminding Angie of how her own mother had looked after her all those years ago.

Twenty minutes later Mrs. Pringle was giving Angie the grand tour of the house, with a constantly running commentary. Although she tried very hard to take in all the information that was being fired at her, it was a huge, rambling old house and eventually the quick-fire details began to blur. Angie could remember there were eight bedrooms, some with dressing rooms attached, several bathrooms, a nursery, a box room and a room for hanging the game but she memorised very little else. As for the layout of the various floors, she was left with no idea where anything was located. The fact that there were two staircases added to the confusion.

As she led the way downstairs, back to ground floor level, Mrs. Pringle said, "I've saved Mr. Anderson's quarters until last. He told me he hoped you would come and instructed me to leave everything just as it was; I wasn't to touch a thing. You see, he wanted you to see for yourself how he lived. Once he was wheelchair-bound, he set about having some of this floor converted into a suite of rooms that were suitable for his needs. He spent most of his time in the studio. I'll take you in there first and leave you to have a look at some of his work. Feel free to wander round any of his rooms; that's what he would have liked. Ring one of the bells if you need me." Off she went, leaving Angie in a large, high-ceilinged room lit by enormous, floor-to-ceiling windows, including a pair of French windows that led out on to a terrace, with a view of the hills beyond.

There was the usual clutter of artists' paints, palette boards, brushes and a couple of easels. Walking over to inspect the work on one of the easels, Angie stopped short with a quick intake of breath. It was a portrait of herself in the midnight blue outfit she'd worn for Rob's exhibition at the gallery; how many years ago? A lot of water had passed under the bridge since then.

She wandered around the room looking through the piles of canvases stacked against the walls. Some of the paintings were of the view from the window at different times of the season but over half of the total paintings he'd left behind included the unmistakeable image of Angie. A few included Rusty at various stages of his young life which had been painted from photographs left pinned to the back to demonstrate how he had such in-depth knowledge of their son. She sorted through pile after pile of skilfully executed paintings but where was the one she so desperately wanted to find? Her searching became more and more frenetic as she skimmed through the canvases, barely looking at them, simply acknowledging it was not the picture she wanted. At last, almost at the end of the collection, she found what she wanted; a self-portrait of Rob, looking just as he did when she had known him, when they were young, vital and so in love. She took it nearer the window, propping it up so that she could see every detail of the face she loved so dearly. Angie fought back the lump in her throat but, once again, she couldn't stop the tears that flowed. After sitting, lost in thought, staring at the portrait, she went back to investigate further that last stack of paintings. Her tenacity was rewarded when she found a composition of the two of them, sitting side by side, the eternity ring on the third finger of her left hand. That was the one she'd take home.

Before taking her leave, Angie took a quick look round the rest of Rob's suite of rooms. The bedroom told the story of his later life, with an electric wheelchair at the side of the bed and a hoist to help him move from the bed to the chair. The bathroom told a similar tale. On the surface, it told of a very different man to the one Angie had known but she could see beyond his tragic illness and its trappings. He was her soul mate who had remained true to her despite life's trials, as she had remained true to him. Not even the relentless, sometimes ruthless, march of time could challenge their love; without question, that was forever.

Returning to the studio, Angie rang the bell to summon Mrs. Pringle. "Thank you for all your help, Mrs. Pringle. I'd like you, your husband and any other staff to know that Rob told me he couldn't have had better people around him during his illness. This has all come as something of a shock to me and I haven't had enough time to think what impact it will have on the future. So, I shall make no hasty decisions and I'll be grateful if everything can continue along the same lines as usual here, at Larchridge, for the time being. I shall keep in touch with you and should you need me, either contact the solicitors or contact me on the telephone number on this card." She passed her business card to Mrs. Pringle, picked up the precious painting and departed.

Roots

Back on the motorway, Angie headed south without having formed any firm plan of action. Contact with Lauren, back at Smart Choice, had confirmed that everything was running smoothly in her absence. Lauren had encouraged her to grab the opportunity to vacation in Europe, an ambition which, apparently, she, herself, had always nursed. Angie's problem was that it was so long since she'd taken time out, she didn't know how to use her new-found freedom. Should she go back to London? Should she visit the Continent? Should she go straight back to L.A. and enjoy some leisure time at home? She was still contemplating the situation when she spotted the signs for Wollingford. Making a snap decision, she turned off the motorway and headed for her old stamping ground.

On her arrival she drove slowly down the main street. Everything looked pretty much the same, with only a few exceptions. The Coliseum Cinema was now a bingo hall, there was a pizza place on the corner of Wellington Road and, further along the main street, a brash, red and yellow sign advertised video's for hire where once the Misses Harrington had sold haberdashery.

The County Hotel, its lovingly-polished brass door-furniture proudly gleaming, had retained its air of good reliable service and hospitality so Angie parked her car and booked in for the night. Once settled in her cosy room with the floral bed cover and pink velvet curtains, she took out her phone to contact her dear, old friend, Reuben, to bring him up to date with her latest activities.

"Hi Angie. Are you still in the U.K.? I've been thinking of you and wondering what that letter was all about. Are you O.K.?"

"Yes, I'm O.K. Yes, I'm still in the U.K. You'll be amazed when I tell you all about that letter from the solicitors." She then proceeded to give him a blow by blow account of everything that had happened since she'd set foot on British soil again.

When she finally paused, Reuben gave a long, slow whistle, then began to chuckle. "I'm sorry, of course, to hear about Rob's dreadful illness, but, I have to say Angie, ever since I've known you, life has never been dull. This kind of thing doesn't happen to other people; it has to be you. What's the next instalment in the saga of Angie Caswell?"

"You can laugh Reuben, but this has all come as quite a shock to me. The question I don't seem to be able to shake is, did I act too hastily? Should I have waited for Rob's explanation? Should I have told him about Rusty? Have I deprived Rusty of the opportunity of knowing his father? It all keeps whirling around, making me feel so horribly guilty."

"I can see where you're coming from Angie but you can't turn back the clock. You made your decision after a lot of careful thought. You did the best you could at that time. You decided, with good reason, that you'd never be able to trust Rob again. They say hindsight is wonderful, but, in my opinion, it can't change a thing. You'll still continue in life doing your best to make the right decision as each new situation arises. You can't do better than that, so stop beating yourself up. Don't forget, Rob too made his own decision not to turn back the clock. He valued the time you had together so highly, he couldn't bear anything to taint it; certainly not his debilitating illness. He also decided that Rusty should have the freedom in his life that he believed he couldn't offer him in his needy, degenerating condition.

No doubt Rob also questioned his decisions over the years but decided to stick with it, balancing the sacrifices he made in not seeing you and Rusty, against the benefits you would gain by not being hindered by him. That was truly an act of love! He knew you so well Angie; he bore no grudge. Move on."

143

"I know I'll have to move on, but first, I'm reconnecting with my roots. I'll try to track down two of my old friends this evening and then tomorrow, I'll visit Millbeck, the village where I was raised. I'll also take the opportunity to visit the church yard where my parents are buried. I've no plans after that."

"That sounds like a good starting point. Knowing you as I do, it won't be long before the plans will come fast and furious. Rob requested you should live for both of you, probably in the knowledge that you wouldn't see any problems in doing just that. I'm of the opinion that your life has reached an important cross road. Take a break, then let me know which direction you choose. Be happy. Have fun." With that, he rang off.

After spending a few minutes considering what Reuben had said, Angie grabbed the phone book, turned to the 'S' section and searched for Skillington. Unsurprisingly, the number was listed under the same address as she'd known as a child. Someone in the family would be able to give her a number for Dennis, if he had moved elsewhere. A female voice, with a strong Derbyshire accent answered the phone. "Hello, is it possible to speak to Dennis Skillington, please?" asked Angie. "Sorry, he's still at the garage. Who's calling? Can I give him a message?"

"You probably won't remember me. My name is Angie Caswell and I was a childhood friend of Dennis. Is it possible to phone him at the garage, or would that be inconvenient for him?"

"Angie Caswell! Of course I remember you. I'm Mandy, his youngest sister. When you grew out of your clothes, you used to pass them on to me. I was so grateful; how could I forget you? Dennis has the garage next to the Post Office here in Millbeck. If you have a pen handy I'll give you his number. He'll be thrilled to bits, hearing from you."

Mandy was right. Dennis was delighted to hear from Angie and arranged to meet her in Wollingford that evening.

"Is Sandra still in the area? It would be great if all three of us could meet up again."

"I haven't seen Sandra in ages. She got married many years ago and moved to Leeds. The next thing I heard was that she was divorced and had taken up with another chap and moved to High Vale. Do you remember High Vale about fifteen miles from here? There's nothing much there but that was the attraction. What I heard was that she wanted to come back here, or to Wollingford, but her mother wouldn't hear of it because of the disgrace so she moved to High Vale where nobody knew her."

"What disgrace? Did she marry a criminal or something?"

"No. Don't you remember? She's a Roman Catholic. Her mother wouldn't forgive her for getting divorced, then when she found out that her second husband was a Hindu that really put the cat amongst the pigeons. The poor woman hardly put her head out of the door because she thought everyone would be pointing the finger and talking about her daughter living in mortal sin with some foreigner."

"And were they gossiping, or did she just imagine it?"

"There's always one or two vicious tongues wagging but most people were too busy getting on with their own lives to bother about what Sandra was doing. I don't know what her married name is so I can't find her in the book. As her mother still lives in Millbeck, I'll call in on my way home and see if she has Sandra's telephone number. She hasn't cut Sandra off altogether, but relations are very frosty."

Later that evening, Angie and Dennis caught up with their news over dinner at the County Hotel.

"So, what happened to your plan to work outdoors on the estate? Did you decide to stay with the cars?"

"No," replied Dennis ruefully, "it wasn't my decision. As they had nobody else locally with the know-how to look after the cars, they kept me dangling, always promising to replace me but never actually doing anything about it. As time went by I decided to capitalise on my skills by working every hour I could to enable me to save enough money to buy my own place. It was hard work because I was the main breadwinner in the house. However, I knew that old Harry Dawson was planning to retire when the lease on his garage in the village came up for renewal; the freehold was owned by Lord Heathleigh, of course. The estate manager wasn't too happy about losing me and tried to put a spanner in the works, if you'll pardon the pun, but old Lord Heathleigh was very fair. He said that as I'd worked hard to buy the business, I should be allowed to take on the lease. With the help of a loan from the bank, I managed and I've been there ever since."

"Good for you. How's it all going? Is it better than working for someone else?" She laughed when she saw his hand rumpling his hair, just as he'd done as a boy when he was unsure of his reply.

"Yes and no. I like being independent in what I do but I haven't been able to carry out my original plan to expand the business. By the time I've paid the bank and the tax man, I just about keep my head above water. Now, I have another problem which I don't think I'm going to be able to resolve. I'll probably lose everything and still end up owing the bank money."

Angie looked concerned, then puzzled. "How can that happen?"

"Well, I take it you do know that Lord Heathleigh passed away, leaving everything to Nick, who isn't even fit to lick his father's boots. He still lives the life of Old Riley over in France with money running through his fingers like water. He has an alcohol problem as well as a huge debt problem and, through no fault of my own, as my lease on the garage is up for renewal again, I've got caught up in his self-induced financial troubles. Because he's so hard up, he's asking for an extortionate sum as a renewal fee, saying it's non-negotiable even though it's a completely unrealistic price. Unlike his son, old Lord Heathleigh was well-aware of how impoverished this area is and he accepted a relatively low purchase price for the lease, knowing it was as much as I could raise. I've managed to put a small amount aside for the renewal, but as I've had to take out further loans with the bank over the years, I'm still in debt to them. I can see no way round it; I'll have to start looking for another job."

"How about the rest of your family? Are they still at home?"

"They've all gone their own way so they're not dependent on me anymore, thank goodness. Mother is frail in body but fiercely independent in spirit. Mandy, who you spoke to on the phone, lives close by with her family and calls round most days to keep an eye on Mother and help out with a few things around the house. She also helps me at the garage by looking after the petrol sales while I'm in the repair shop."

"I plan to visit Millbeck tomorrow. I'll go to Mum and Dad's grave, then I'll call round and see you at the garage. Meantime, I'll put on my thinking cap; we can't let Nick get away with this. There's got to be something we can do. The last time I saw him was at his eighteenth birthday party. What a fiasco that was!"

"Never to be forgotten," grinned Dennis. "Have you heard about Godly's career?"

"Don't tell me he's followed his father into the Church, or perhaps, he's made a fortune working in the City?"

"Neither of those; he's in fish and chips."

"You always were an awful kidder Dennis Skillington. Godfrey Hoddlestone in fish and chips? Come off it."

"Seriously, do you remember that shy, rather plain girl in the year below us? Janet Wilson was her name. Her family ran the chip shop on Beck Row. Well Godly had been doing his Romeo bit with her, buying her flowers, taking her out in his father's car, etc. The poor girl had never caught the eye of any other boy and was completely swept off her feet by the attention he gave her. Apparently she was telling her parents that she was elsewhere, the cinema or meeting friends, when it was fairly common knowledge that most evenings Godly's car was parked up at Drover's Ridge with steamy windows. Of course, when someone told her family, the balloon went up good and proper. Those two burly brothers of hers were waiting for them to park up again. When the windows began to steam up, they dragged Godly out of the car, with his trousers around his ankles in a most undignified fashion. They threatened him but their somewhat dishevelled sister got in between them to defend loverboy.

Terrified but unharmed, Godly was unceremoniously taken home by Brothers Wilson to meet their parents; I'm not sure who was the scariest, their father or their mother. Janet wept and wailed, telling them how sorry she was but she couldn't help herself because she loved him and wanted to marry him. Seeing Godfrey as quite a good catch for his wallflower of a daughter, Mr. Wilson made him an offer he couldn't refuse. He pointed out that his irresponsible behaviour could have got his virtuous daughter in the family way; who was to know that hadn't already happened? Therefore, he should do the right thing by marrying her, as soon as possible, to save her reputation. Knowing that Godfrey wasn't working, being between university and an undecided future, Mr. and Mrs. Wilson offered to start them off on their path to wedded bliss with the present of a fish and chip shop business. They'd had their eye on suitable premises in Wollingford for some time."

Choking with laughter, Angie said, "Had Godfrey ever been in a fish and chip shop? He'd led a very refined lifestyle; not like the rest of us."

"Terror is an extremely powerful motivator," remarked Dennis drolly. "He might not have known anything about fish and chips then, but he was a quick learner. He and Janet were married hastily but with all the usual pomp and ceremony, then they quickly set about opening up their business. The whole place was done out in a black and gold theme and called 'Posh shoP'. They bought a motor scooter so that Godly could deliver posh fish and chips to the door, while Janet cooked in the shop.

"How was that posh?"

"Oh! It was certainly posher than any other fish and chip establishment in the area. Nothing was wrapped in paper. They used insulated cartons and for home deliveries they included a pack of condiments, cutlery and a gold coloured serviette. Everything had the word "posh" printed on it. They had two or three tables in the shop so that you could be served on the premises if you wanted to dine out for the evening, but it was the delivery service that was the making of them. It took off like wild fire, especially when they started advertising that they would deliver at home for 'Posh' fish and chip parties. It became all the rage because it was something different. They did so well, they opened more shops across the county. If you're here any length of time you'll see their fleet of vans running around, black with golden 'Posh' along the side."

"Well, who would have dreamt that all that expensive education would come in handy in establishing a train of posh fish and chip shops? Was Janet pregnant?"

"It would seem not. In fact, they've never had a family. Perhaps that was because they never returned to steam up car windows at Drovers Ridge; they were too busy building their Posh empire."

"I suppose Mr. and Mrs. Wilson are very proud of their son-in-law, but what of Revd. and Mrs. Hoddlestone? What do they think about it all?"

"They beat a hasty retreat to do evangelical work in some far-flung corner of the globe. I haven't heard about them in years. Anyway, enough of them. What's your story Angie? What have you been up to since we last met?"

Angie had been laughing so much at the way Dennis had told the tale, she had tears of mirth rolling down her face. Dabbing her eyes, she replied, "I guess my proudest achievement is my son, Rusty. He's twenty years old and he's travelling Europe with his friends at the moment."

"So! You finally found a Mr. Wonderful and allowed him to be your husband?"

"I said I had a son. I can't remember saying anything about marriage."

"Oh! Immaculate Conception then? There's been one or two of them around here over the years." That started Angie giggling again.

"Well, there's nothing much changed about you, I'm glad to say. You're still the same old Dennis in essence, but I have to admit that your wit, perhaps, has improved."

Over coffee, they returned to the thorny subject of the garage lease. Angie arranged to meet Dennis next morning and promised to give the matter some long, hard thought in the meantime. "I don't see what you can do," said Dennis with a resigned shrug of his shoulders, "but if it means spending more time with you before you go home, then I'm up for it. I've missed you Angie."

"I've missed you more than I realized, Dennis." They hugged and went their separate ways.

The Garage

There was an air of peace in the little church yard as Angie relaxed on the wooden bench, close to her parents' grave, where she'd placed a posy of pink roses. They'd been good parents, happy parents, gone from this world but her memories of them would never die. They'd live forever in her heart. She stayed a while, happily letting her mind wander down memory lane until, glancing at her wrist watch, she sighed, blew them both a kiss, and walked toward the gate, ready to deal with the matters of the day.

She headed towards the garage to discuss business problems with Dennis, finding him bright and cheerful as ever despite being desperately worried about the situation. In addition to his financial burden, his mother, physically frail but indomitable in spirit, was declining rapidly, requiring more intensive daily care.

"First of all," Angie asked Dennis, "do you have a copy of your lease or is it with your bank? If I'm to help you I need to see it."

"I have a copy at home. I'll ask Mandy if she can drop it round here for you."

"Secondly. Show me around and then tell me what your original plans were to extend the business. Also, would you mind if I had a look at your books?"

"You don't do things by half, do you? I hadn't expected all this but I can see, you've really given it a lot of thought. There's not much to show you, just a reception area, a tiny office, and a ramshackle old shed outside that acts as a workshop. Come and see."

After a quick inspection, Angie asked, "Is there no toilet facility on the premises? I see there's a sink in your office; does it have a hot water supply?"

Dennis smiled wryly. "It's owned by the estate so what do you expect? You know their reputation is not good when it comes to looking after their tenants. Nothing has been done here since before I became tenant, despite my complaints. They've got me over a barrel. There was an old, outside toilet round the back when I first came here which wasn't connected to the main sewerage system. They promised they would build a simple, modern facility attached to the mains but I'm still waiting. When we need hot water, we boil a kettle. It's not much here, I know, but it's all I've got and if I lose it, I have nothing at all."

"If you had the money, what would you do to improve the business?"

"That's a big IF. IF a miracle should happen, I'd reorganise the reception area, moving the counter forward to make a smaller public space but more room to transfer the office equipment into the area behind the counter. If there was enough money left over, I'd buy a computer. If there was even more money, I'd extend the current office space to provide a small kitchen-type area with a fridge, sink and microwave and then I'd attach two outside toilets, one private for staff and one for the public." Dennis shrugged his shoulders and gave Angie one of his endearing grins. "Everyone has to have a dream, I suppose."

"Most things are possible, Dennis; you just have to work out how to make them happen. I need some contacts of mine to look over your lease. Would you object if I faxed them a copy through the hotel fax machine?"

"Not at all. I trust you implicitly, if you want to spend your time on it. I don't think it will change anything, but if you want to have a go, feel free."

"We shall see, oh, ye of little faith. I'll be back in two days' time after I've had time to look into a few things. Meanwhile, it's about time you did some work around here." She skipped out of the door, narrowly escaping an oily rag her friend had lobbed at her.

True to her word, Angie returned two days later. Mandy was behind the counter, giving Dennis and Angie an opportunity to settle down in the office to go through the huge sheaf of paperwork she'd brought with her.

"I've been a very busy girl," Angie told her friend. "I have so much to tell you, I don't know where to start. Perhaps I should start with the unknown element in all this. How much is Nick asking for the renewal of your lease?"

"Fifty thousand pounds for fifteen years plus a monthly rental of fifty pounds."

"Wow, he's really pushing his luck, trying for that kind of money in such a poor area. I've found out quite a lot about Mr. Nick in the last two days and he is genuinely up the old proverbial creek without a paddle. He's massively overspent with no place left to find help. Things are so bad, he's trying to sell Holliwell Hall."

"Never," exploded her friend in disbelief. How could he?"

"With great difficulty," replied Angie. "He's stripped it of everything that had any value and is left with a massive white elephant, apart from the land. I'm telling you this in strictest confidence, Dennis, but the investigators I've had on the job have assured me that the only people who have shown any interest are a theme park development company."

"Not a theme park," moaned Dennis. "Not here in our lovely, old Millbeck. It'll be the ruination of the place."

"Put your business cap on Dennis. It could be the making of the place. You know how many younger people are leaving to earn money elsewhere. Well, just think, a theme park would bring a lot of employment with it. Nothing stays the same for ever, except for those hills up there." She waved in the direction of the slopes they'd wandered as children.

"It may surprise you to know that I'm looking for somewhere to invest some money of mine and it would give me a perverse pleasure to get one over on Nick. I haven't forgotten how he tried to patronise me in the past; well, the boot's on the other foot now but we need to act quickly. I have a proposal for you."

"I'm not marrying you," he chirped.

"Despite that bitter blow," she continued coolly, "I propose that I become your business partner; it won't contravene any conditions in your lease. I've set up an investment company called 'Esther Smith Finance', which I'll use to buy into your business, if you agree to the plan. Nick won't know it's me who's financing you but he will recognize the London solicitors and the City investment bank who'll be contacting him. He won't mess them around like he does his tenants.

My solicitors have scrutinized the lease and have found the landlord to be lacking in keeping to his side of the deal. The Estate contracted to keep the buildings to a good standard and to contact the tenant every five years to discuss necessary maintenance matters, such as electrical rewiring etc. They've fallen down on several issues. Knowing how desperate Nick is for cash, I propose that we refuse to renew the lease."

As Dennis opened his mouth to speak, she said, "Just a minute. I suggest that, instead, we make an offer of £30,000 for the freehold of this place. If he accepts, we'll waive our rights to sue him for compensation for his breach of contract over the past several years, otherwise we'll have to look at legal redress. That will scare the pants off him. Also, he'll probably be eager to grab any cash that comes his way, even if it is only peanuts compared with his total debts."

Dennis looked mystified. "Why are you doing this Angie? You've seen the accounts so you must know it'll

154

take years for you to recover that kind of investment? Another thing; how much do you expect me to cough up for the freehold?"

"I've already told you, I'm looking for somewhere to invest. Trust me Dennis, when I tell you that there's going to be big changes in Millbeck and we're going to be in at the beginning before prices increase. Nick is on his uppers and needs to jump before he's pushed and I have it from a reliable source that there's a good chance the theme park will go ahead. I'm not sure what will happen to all the other properties he owns around here but he may be put into a position where he'll have to sell those too in order to raise funds. If so, people like your mother and Mandy could receive an opportunity to buy at a very low price because they're sitting tenants."

"I can understand about the house, but I still can't understand why this garage is a good investment for you." Dennis sat rumpling the top of his head.

"Let me explain my idea in full. Once the theme park is up and running, it'll bring a lot of tourists into this village; we can cash in on that. Not only will we completely modernise the building in the way that you've suggested, but we'll also review how the business operates. The garage stands on quite a good plot of land, much of which is under-used at present. We could extend the main building slightly to make room for a shop area, selling snacks, drinks etc. Outside we could clear a spot for a couple of picnic tables where tourists can either bring their own food or buy refreshments from the shop. In time, we could possibly buy a few bikes for hire. Another idea would be to organize guided walks, capitalising on your in-depth knowledge of the area. What do you think?"

"You amaze me Angie. You make it all sound so simple, but where's the money coming from? Apart from the purchase price, the development would take money. I can't see the bank giving us a loan; it would be too risky for them."

"Between you, me and these four walls, Dennis, I can afford it. You and I can sort out shares and payments once we're up and running."

"What if the scheme doesn't work? What if it flops?"

"There's always that chance, of course, but on the other hand, what if it's a great, big, fat success? If it fails, we're left with a property that has a value and a business that is worthless. In that case I'll probably lose money but you won't be any worse off than you are at present. I love a challenge and I'm prepared to take the risk. What about you?"

"I'd love to have a go, but I really can't afford it Angie. All I have in the world is £10,000 I'd scrimped and scraped to renew the lease. If we're to be partners in the property, I'd need another £5,000 and I know for sure that the bank won't lend me any more until I've cleared my current loan."

"That's not a problem. You don't need to go to the bank. I'll make you a loan of £5,000 and, what's more, I'll clear your bank loan. We can then set up a financial arrangement whereby you repay me over a set period of time at an interest rate which will be much lower than the bank's."

"Why are you doing this Angie?"

"You're my friend Dennis, a very special friend who I know I can trust and depend on through thick and thin. I choose to do it because I can and because I'll just love being involved in this project with you."

"Come here," he said gruffly, opening his arms out wide. Happy, in the comfort of his big bear hug, she said eventually, "Will you marry me now?"

Setting her free, he grinned widely, saying "No, but I'll accept your other proposal. Let's do it Angie."

"Hooray," she whooped, holding out her hand. "Let's go for it!"

Reuben

"Hi Reuben. It's Angie. How's it going?"

"Hi Angie. Good to hear from you; I think that English accent is getting a little stronger. What have you been up to since we last talked? How's everything going with the garage project? Has the purchase been completed yet?"

"Wow! Hold your fire, that's a lot of questions. Yes, my guys put pressure on Nick, telling him they needed an answer in double-quick time or the offer would be withdrawn. We've got the builders in, revamping the current buildings and we've submitted a planning application to the local planning department for permission to expand for the proposed shop. It's so exciting.

What have you been up to? Did you make a decision on whether or not to retire?"

Reuben groaned. "Yep, I've decided I don't want to retire and Rebekah has decided that I most certainly will retire to spend more time with her and the rest of the family. The best compromise I can reach is to work half-day Friday and stay home on Mondays. It's not working out too badly but I know there's no way I can retire; it's unthinkable. I thrive on business and full-time retirement would be like a death sentence."

"I can sympathise with you on that. I'm enjoying being a free agent on a temporary basis but I love the buzz business gives me; it's like food and drink."

"So, what will you do Angie? Will you go back to Smart Choice or will you concentrate on your business in the U.K.?"

"I'm not too sure. As far as the agency is concerned, Lauren seems to have everything under control and I realize, having been away from it for a while, it's not challenging me like it used to in the early days. I feel as though everything has changed around me and I'm uncertain which path I should choose.

What's weighing heavily on my mind is that I haven't told Rusty about the will yet. He's coming to the U.K. in three weeks' time on the final lap of his tour of Europe, when I'd like to take him to Larchridge as I feel it's a part of his birth-right and I'd like to show him the letter in those surroundings. Needless to say, although I'm dying to show him the place, at the same time I'm dreading it. What will he say when he learns his father has died without ever meeting him? Will he be angry with me? Will he hate me? I feel so guilty as far as he's concerned."

"Don't forget, it wasn't just your decision. Rob cared enough about him to get regular reports and photographs but he decided he didn't want anyone to share his life as an invalid. He made that decision because he cared about you and Rusty. Whether Rusty is mature enough yet to understand is open to question, but he's a good boy; he'll get it if you give him enough time. What's the plan for the rest of your stay in the U.K.?"

"What would I do without you Reuben? As a matter of fact I have made a plan. This evening I shall meet Dennis for dinner, together with the other member of our childhood gang of three; my friend Sandra. It's years since I've seen her and I can't tell you how much I'm looking forward to catching up with her again. So far, I haven't made any other firm plans."

Reuben chuckled. "So far, Angie, so far. Let me know when the next plan surfaces in that active brain of yours. What would I do without you? Your energy is inspirational. Have fun this evening. Bye." He was gone and Angie turned her thoughts towards dinner with Dennis and Sandra.

Friends

Sitting in the corner of the lounge at the County Hotel, chatting with Dennis, Angie kept a vigilant eye on the doorway. Would she recognize Sandra? Would she have changed much? Mrs. Bennett had seemed quite bitter and spoke of her daughter as though she'd turned out to be a 'scarlet woman'. Would she actually turn up as promised? Angie needn't have worried. When a slim, smartly-dressed brunette with shining, shoulder-length hair stepped through the doorway wearing a familiar, enquiring look on her face, they recognized each other immediately. Angie got to her feet, waving to her friend, while Sandra rushed across the room to fling her arms around her old pal. Dennis, too, stood up, holding out his arms. "Isn't anyone going to give me a hug?" he asked. "I'm a friend too."

The years quickly disappeared as their easy conversation became increasingly animated while they caught up with each other's news, then merrily meandered down Memory Lane. They were still the same close-knit trio they'd been so many years ago.

"I've never laughed so much in ages," said Sandra, towards the end of the evening. "It's just fantastic being with you two again." Turning to Angie, she asked, "What are your plans now that you've helped Dennis re-organize his garage? How long will you be around here?"

"Well, I haven't quite finished at the garage. There's one more idea I'd like to throw at Dennis."

He pulled a face. "I hardly dare ask what it is. You're not going to propose to me again, are you?"

"You've got it, bang on. I propose that when we launch the new premises, we call the business 'Skillington Stop', being sure to include somewhere in the blurb that the proprietors are Dennis Skillington and Angie Caswell. Before you start your questions, let me explain my reasoning behind it. Skillington Stop sounds more like a tourist destination than simply somewhere to fill up your petrol tank; it might encourage people to make more use of the other services we provide. Also, I want our names in the public eye so that Nick will learn exactly who owns the land and business. I know that's petty and I'm not going to make any excuses. He tolerated us as village children but always looked down his nose at us. He probably always will, but, in my pathetic way, I'll just feel we've had some redress."

"That's a great idea," beamed Sandra. "You'll have to vote with us Skillington, because you're already out-voted two out of three."

"I'm not sure how you became entitled to a vote," joked Dennis, "but I'll go along with it. Anything for a quiet life. Skillington Stop it is."

"Do you have any other plans, Angie?" enquired Sandra.

"Yes. Recent events have made me acutely aware that the years are galloping by at an alarming rate so I've decided I should do some of the things I've always wanted to do but never actually got round to because I was always so busy. I don't want to look back with regret when I'm old and decrepit."

"Serious stuff," remarked Dennis. "Dare I ask what's at the top of your list?"

"You might well ask, because it involves you."

Dennis groaned at the thought of it. "What is it now?" he asked warily.

"I've always wanted to go up on the hills in the evening to see the badger setts. I wasn't allowed to go when I was a child but there's no one to stop me now. Would you take me Dennis? It would genuinely be one of my dreams come true."

"And me," joined in Sandra enthusiastically. "Go on Dennis. I promise to be as quiet as a Trappist monk." They all sniggered.

"How can I refuse? Why would I refuse? When do you want to go girls? I can do any evening except Friday."

A few days later, the three friends were relaxing behind a drink in the Weavers Arms, at Millbeck. "That was magical Dennis, every bit as good as I'd ever dreamed of." "Yes," agreed Sandra, "it was like entering another world. It might sound dramatic but I felt kind of privileged to be there, watching them in their private moonlit world. Thank you Dennis. You're the greatest." The two women raised their glasses to the cheerfully grinning Dennis.

"What would you do, Dennis, if you could make a dream come true?" asked Sandra.

"My dream has come true. I'm freed from the ties with the estate and I believe our business has real prospects. What more could I want?"

"I'm glad you feel liberated by throwing off the shackles of feudalism. Also, good news regarding those business prospects; my contacts confirmed today that Nick has definitely agreed to sell Holliwell Hall to the development company. What would you do if you could, Sandra?" asked Angie.

"I'd go to Rome to see the Pope." Dennis stared in amazement but didn't utter a word.

"Why would you want to do that?" asked Angie. "I know you're Catholic but why is it so important to see the Pope?"

"Well, I'd really like to confess my sins to him and ask for forgiveness. I'd feel kind of cleansed."

"This is getting too deep for me," said Dennis. "Drink up girls, the barman's yawning.

Sandra

Next afternoon, Angie rang Sandra. "Glad to find you at home. I've been thinking about what you said last night, about your dream of seeing the Pope. Dennis and I have both had a dream come true and I thought it would be great if it worked for you too. I've been making a few enquiries."

"I don't believe you Angie Caswell. You never give up. How can I possibly visit the Pope?"

"It's possible for you to see the Pope but we can't arrange for him to take your confession. He comes onto his balcony every Wednesday in St. Peter's Square to address the public, so it would be possible for you to join in with all those other devoted Catholics. I'm afraid I can't manage to get you an individual audience with the Pope, but couldn't you just visit some other church in Rome and confess your sins?"

"You're amazing but how do you propose I get there? Where would I stay? It'll be very expensive and I'm a bit hard-up at the moment because I've helped fund my daughter Asha's trip to India."

"So that would leave you and your husband?"

"Who? Prem? I don't think so, Angie. Prem's a Hindu, besides which he's currently back in India helping sort out the family affairs after his mother's death last month. It's a bone of contention at the moment because he can't give me a date for his return. He's a sociology lecturer and as the new academic year starts at the end of September, he'll need to return by then but he's a bit short on the specifics right now. Meantime, I'm here on my own, except for the few hours I still work for my mobile beauty business. I'm fed-up, rattling around this lonely house without Prem or Asha and I was thinking of suggesting you might like to spend a few days with me, if you're going to be around here a bit longer."

"That's very kind of you Sandra. Thank you. We'll have a look at some dates because I'm expecting Rusty to come and spend a couple of days with me when he visits the U.K. Meanwhile, what if I book us a trip to Rome for Monday? We could do our tourist thing for a couple of days, see the Pope's appearance in the square on Wednesday, and then fly home. I had a bit of luck recently, so the trip is on me. Are you up for it?"

"Oh! That does sound like a dream come true. Are you sure? It's very generous of you."

"You can repay me by styling my hair for me. I don't want the Holy Father to see me in my current unruly state. I'll ring you back when I've firmed up the arrangements. Ciao!"

Three days later the pair booked into a boutique hotel in the heart of Rome. Sandra rushed around their room, looking into all the doors and drawers, inspecting the bathroom, the bed, the minibar and, finally, the magnificent view over Rome.

"I can't believe I'm actually here," she said excitedly. "I haven't been abroad for years. To be here, in Rome where everything is so beautiful is just amazing, especially when this time last week it was just a pipe dream I never thought would really come to anything. Where shall we go first? Trevi Fountain to make a wish? You choose."

The two friends spent the afternoon soaking up the sun, perched on the edge of the Trevi Fountain watching the world go by. Later, they took a taxi up to the Roman hills for dinner. Relaxing in the cool window area with long white curtains fluttering in the evening breeze, they watched in wonder as the sun went down on the distant horizon in all its fiery magnificence.

Next day, they donned their walking shoes and visited as many tourist spots as they could manage in the time available, returning to spend another evening in the cool, elegant restaurant high up in the hills.

On Wednesday morning Angie awoke to find Sandra dressed and ready for her visit to St. Peter's Square.

"Today's event really does mean a lot to you, doesn't it?" she observed.

Sandra nodded in wholehearted agreement. "Yes, it certainly does. Afterwards, I shall find a church and ask if someone will take my confession. After all, that is the underlying purpose of this visit. I want to confess my sins fully."

Shaking her head, Angie regarded her earnest friend. "I can't even imagine what these sins could be to make you feel so guilty. You're not a mass murderer are you, with bodies stashed under the back lawn?"

"It's no joke," protested Sandra. "I can't tell you everything but every time I visit Mother she reminds me that I'm living in sin."

"Aren't you married to Prem?"

"As far as the law is concerned, I'm married to him but as far as the Church, and my mother, are concerned I'm living in sin."

"Why? I don't understand."

"My first husband was Roman Catholic and, of course, we intended to remain married for life. Sadly, it didn't quite work out that way and we were divorced, but the Church doesn't recognize the end of our marriage unless we go through a church process to try to obtain an annulment. If they decide our original intent was to stay married for life, then they won't grant us an annulment. I can't, in all honesty, say that my original marriage intentions weren't for life. Neither could my first husband. They just changed along the way."

"So, where does that leave you?"

"In the eyes of the law I'm legally divorced and married to Prem. However, in the eyes of the Church, I'm married to Robert until one of us dies and currently I'm committing an adulterous act towards him by living as a wife with Prem."

"But weren't you aware of all this when you married Prem? What happened? The other thing is, why did you and your husband get divorced when you had vowed to stay together for life?"

"Ah, that's a complicated story. I'll try to tell you, quickly, because I want to arrive in the Square early enough to get a good view of his Holiness. I mustn't be late.

I met Robert when I was quite young. He was so dashing and so different from any of the other men I knew. Mother warned me not to marry in haste, but we were both in love with the idea of being in love, got married in a rush and went to live in Leeds because he worked in London and travelled to and fro by train, so Leeds was convenient. Also, I had no problem in finding a new job in a salon in Leeds."

"So if your mother was against it from the start, what did his parents think of a whirlwind marriage?"

"I'm not sure. His mother had died and his father was convalescing somewhere in the Caribbean after a serious illness."

"Anyway, to continue my tale. Like most young couples, it was all very romantic to begin with and things went well until his work started to keep him away from home, initially for short periods, but soon I was left on my own for longer and longer periods of time. The pressure was well and truly switched on when he became involved in a big project his company set up in America and I began to see less and less of him.

I started to feel quite depressed as it reminded me of my childhood when Mother spent so much time on her own. Do you remember how my father was never around because he was always away at sea? She became increasingly resentful about it so that when he did come home, they rowed all the time. Eventually, Dad stopped coming back at all, took up with another woman and raised a family. Mother, of course, remained faithful but very, very lonely.

I was at quite a low ebb when along came Prem. Handsome, sensitive, considerate Prem. He was a lecturer at Leeds University, new to this country without any friends. We met accidentally in a coffee bar and just started chatting. Although conversation between us was easy, we never dreamt how our relationship would progress. We tried very hard to keep it platonic because I was married, and, also, he didn't want to become emotionally involved with a female who wasn't of the Hindu faith, but one thing led to another. We saw each other more and more frequently until we reached a point where we couldn't live without each other. Everything about this relationship was so much more intense than anything I'd ever experienced when I was younger. We became lovers and the next thing we knew I was pregnant, which would have been wonderful if it were not for the fact that I was married to someone else.

I decided I would have to take the bull by the horns and discuss the situation with my husband, who was working in America. He was a staunch Roman Catholic and I didn't think he would take too kindly to my unfaithful behaviour. I knew, without any doubt, the infatuation of my youth had disappeared, leaving me with a positive, burning desire to spend the rest of my life with Prem, whatever that would take. Somehow, I needed to convince my husband he should divorce me. I was prepared to use all my powers of persuasion, so I booked a flight to go out to talk to him in person thinking that would probably be more effective than a telephone conversation.

When I arrived, he was his usual polite self but somehow seemed a bit more remote than usual. Immediately, I felt guilty, thinking he'd guessed what I was about to say. I was all keyed up to tell him and persuade him to agree to a divorce but I didn't get a chance. Imagine my surprise when he told me that he'd intended getting in touch with me because he had something of grave importance to tell me. Get this, Angie; he had the nerve to tell me he'd been having an affair, wanted to marry the woman and begged me to agree to a divorce.

I hit the roof. I'd been racked with guilt and worry when all that time, he'd been living with someone else. Again, it brought back all the memories of Mother and Father, enough to make me dig my heels in and refuse. I don't know what came over me because I was cutting off my nose to spite my face. Something just made me refuse repeatedly. I've never been so angry in my life.

He took me away for a few days break in the hope that we could calm down and discuss things rationally but the deceit I'd suffered created this vicious, overpowering urge to hurt him. He apologised, he accepted all the blame, he said the woman in question was unaware of his marriage and he offered me very generous financial settlements. None of it was to any avail; I flew home without making any agreement, ready to weep on Prem's shoulder."

"What did Prem think about it all?"

"He sympathised with me at first, then he gradually persuaded me to re-think our situation. We couldn't get married unless I was divorced and there was the inescapable fact that our baby was on the way. Of course, once I'd calmed down, I could see the situation more clearly. I got in touch with Robert, told him I would agree to a divorce and would accept the financial settlement he proposed. I don't know where he was going to get the money from because he didn't earn much of a salary but that wasn't my problem."

"Didn't you ever tell him about Prem and the baby?"

"No. I was mean enough to let him carry on thinking he was the only guilty party."

"That wasn't like you Sandra. Haven't you ever regretted that over the years?"

"Yes, I have and that's one of the things I want to confess. I feel so ashamed and it perpetually weighs heavily on my conscience. I should have let him know that I accepted an equal share of the blame for our break-up." Sandra paused, looking at the watch on her wrist.

"Oh, dear. Is that the time? We'll have to get going." She looked over to where Angie was sitting quietly. "Are you alright, Angie? You look unusually pale."

"Yes. No. I don't know." With that, Angie fled to the bathroom where she was violently sick. She staggered back with difficulty and flopped onto the bed.

"Whatever's brought this on?" asked Sandra anxiously. "Can I get you a drink of water or something? Do you think it's something you ate?"

"Don't worry. I'll be O.K. shortly, if I can just lie here quietly. I'm sorry but I don't think I'm going to be able to make it to St. Peter's Square; I feel slightly dizzy and my legs are wobbly. The staff in Reception will get you a taxi to take you right up to the spot. You're going to have to do this without me."

Left on her own, Angie lay on the bed, everything Sandra had just told her spinning around in her head. Thinking back to that last evening she'd spent with Rob, she remembered the voice on the phone. 'Is Robert there, please?' She knew now without a shadow of doubt, that voice was Sandra's. Then there was the vision of Rob greeting his 'mother' in the twilight. The elegant lady with the long dark hair had been Sandra.

Shocked, she lay there in semi-darkness, trying to work out what it all meant, until, exhausted, she reached for her handbag, took out her wallet and extracted a photograph. She looked at it intently for a few minutes, then kissed it and slipped it under her pillow before curling up and shutting out the world by falling into the welcome oblivion of sleep. She knew no more until she was awakened by the sound of a door closing; Sandra had returned.

"Oh, you're awake. How are you feeling now?" She busied around, raising the blinds to allow the bright sunshine to flood the room.

"I'm feeling a bit better. How did you get on? Did you see his Holiness? Did you go to confession somewhere?"

"Yes and no. I managed to get a place near the front; there were hundreds of people, including loads of nuns. It was very exciting waiting amongst that huge crowd in the grip of what can only be described as euphoric anticipation, and then they all went crazy as he finally appeared on the balcony, a small figure in white robes. It was at that point that it happened."

"What happened?"

"I experienced the strangest, the most life-changing moment of my entire existence. I looked to see the leader of our church, God's holy representative on earth, but was astonished to find I simply saw a man before me; a mere mortal, of human flesh and blood. The aura surrounding his being, that hallowed, divine mystique, floated away into non-existence before my very gaze. "

"What were you expecting to see?"

"I'm not sure but I did expect to feel something extraordinary. There's no doubt it was extraordinary but not in the way I'd anticipated; there was just this mighty, overwhelming, gut-wrenching sensation of anti-climax. He was only a man, of human form and frailties, waving to an ecstatic, cheering crowd. It was as though someone had ripped the blindfold from my eyes, allowing me to see clearly for the first time in my life."

"What did you do then? Did you go to confession?"

"I wandered around for a bit, thinking about what I told you this morning, thinking about Mother's miserable, lonely life, wondering what was the point of it all. How could some priest I've never even met before possibly understand what has gone on in my life? He's probably experienced nothing other than a life in the Church, yet it's men like him, well-meaning no doubt, who make the rules that affect my life. They exercise a steely control over people like me, built on fear and guilt, which I've never dared to question. Voicing such thoughts would only confirm the fact that I'm a sinner. Suddenly, it didn't make sense any more. I decided to go into the first church I came across to talk it over with God; I know, I know, cutting out the middle man but it helped me get my head straight. I still have my faith and kneeling there, I felt the strong, spiritual atmosphere of that church and knew God was with me. He helped me realize that the person to whom I should be making the confession is Robert. He's the one who should know what I did. Until I do that, I'll always feel guilty."

"It's too late now, Sandra."

"What do you mean? Too late?"

"Come over here, I've something to tell you." Angie patted a space on the bed. "Take a look at this," she said, taking the photograph from under her pillow.

As Sandra looked at the photo, a puzzled expression crossed her face. "This is you and Robert. How on earth did you know him? I don't understand. Why do you say it's too late to tell him the truth?"

"I knew him when I worked in New York. I'm sorry to give you the bad news, but Robert is dead." There was a silence while Sandra tried to digest the information.

"When did that happen?" Without waiting for a reply, she continued. "Just when I'd decided to tell him the truth, this happens. I was going to try to find him; I'm not sure how, but I was going to give it a go. Now I'll never be able to tell him."

"That's sad," sympathised Angie, "but at least you can be proud that you really did intend contacting him to make a clean breast of it to him. That's cold comfort, but it's something to hang on to, isn't it?"

Sandra pulled a face, shrugging her shoulders.

Angie took a deep breath. "This seems to be the big day for confessions Sandra. It's my turn to tell you something now, the truth of which I've only just discovered myself and I'm still trying to come to terms with it. The fact is, I knew your ex-husband very well indeed. I knew him as Rob but didn't know anything about his background. I certainly didn't know he was married when I fell head over heels in love with him and planned to spend the rest of my life with him."

"What?" shrieked Sandra. "Did he know how you felt about him?"

Angie went on to tell her the full story, finishing with a description of how she'd come over to the U.K. to see the London solicitors because they wanted to give her a letter which Rob had specified should be handed over in person. She didn't mention that she'd also inherited his property and wealth, thinking that might be indelicate in the circumstances, being just too much for Sandra to digest along with all the other information that had been sprung on her.

Sandra moved across the room to sit in a chair by the window. She kept repeating, "I don't believe it. I don't believe it. How could that happen? You of all people?"

Angie fell quiet. Soon, an uncomfortable silence fell on the room as each of the two friends were lost in their own private thoughts. Eventually, Sandra got to her feet, to pace back and forth like a caged tiger. Finally, she asked, "Now that you know the truth, do you hate me?" She turned an anguished face towards the motionless figure on the bed. "If I hadn't been so spiteful, so selfish, your life would have been very different. I spoilt everything for you."

"I don't seriously think I could ever hate you Sandra. Why should you have known, or even believed, the 'other woman' was unaware that Rob was married? Who's to say how I would have reacted when I discovered the truth about his marital status? The past is what it is. Nothing we can do can change that. Rob has gone to his rest; no more pain and suffering for him. I'm left with Rusty, who's the centre of my world, and you have Prem and Asha. We have to move on; easier said than done, I know. What do you think about it all? Can you ever forgive me?"

"It's difficult to think straight after such a shock, especially coming on top of my weird revelation in St. Peter's Square. What a day! However, I think, perhaps, if I'd still loved Robert, I'd probably find it difficult to forgive you, even though you didn't actually know he was married, but the truth is, that first flush of our young love was well and truly over by then. It was honestly nothing to do with love, because, instead, it was my pride that got in the way of everything. I couldn't face the fact that he'd met someone he liked more than me. Although I didn't want him any longer, I didn't want anyone else to have him. I don't blame you for any of it. It was my fault for acting like a pathetic, selfish, jealous fool. Also, I think Robert was at fault for not telling you the truth earlier in your relationship."

"Let's not play the blame game," suggested Angie. "It won't change a thing. The burning question is, how shall we continue? Are we able to put it behind us and remain friends?"

"It all feels rather strange, I have to admit, but how could we not be friends? It's hard to believe, but I feel closer to you than ever after the events of the last couple of days. Come on Angie Caswell. Give me a hug, then pack your bag. We have a plane to catch."

Revelation for Rusty

"Hi, Reuben. How are things with you?"

"I'm good, Angie. Where are you? Still in the U.K.?"

"Still here. Rusty landed in London this morning and is currently on a train coming north to meet his old mom, who's both incredibly excited and scared at the same time."

"How so? I can understand the excitement, but why scared?"

"I'm taking him to Larchridge today to show him where his father lived and died. He doesn't know a thing about what was in the will and I'm scared about how he'll take the news that Rob has died without ever meeting him. Rusty's entitled to be angry with both of us. We haven't exactly been conventional parents."

"Stop worrying. It's a different generation Angie. He's grown up amongst kids who come from all sorts of family backgrounds. At least he's had a happy childhood, which is more than a lot of his friends can say. Once he gets over the initial shock, he'll pick himself up and get on with his life. Before you know where you are, he'll be telling you all about his adventures in Europe; that's what's important to him. You'll see."

A nervous Angie waited in the car park for the train from London to arrive. Fortunately she didn't have to wait long before she spotted the tall, handsome young man with the heavy backpack loping through the exit, eagerly looking to right and left, trying to find a face he recognized. She waved frantically, running towards him for that big bear hug he always gave her. "It's ages since I last saw you," she said, leading him towards her hire car. "I've missed you."

He grinned mischievously. "It must be a long time Mom; you've developed an English accent. Very impressive." Angie started up the car. "Yes, and I've become quite skilful at driving on the left-hand side of the road too."

"Are you going to tell me where we're going? You sounded quite mysterious on the phone. Also, you haven't told me yet about the solicitors you came to see. You just kind of passed over it quickly but didn't tell me any of the details."

"There's quite a bit to tell you Rusty so try to be patient. First of all, do you remember when we first read the solicitors' letter, you joked that Lord something or other may have left us something in his will? Well, you were right first time."

"Quit joking Mom. Tell me the truth."

"It's no joke. However, before you get carried away on that issue, there is a serious side to all this. Let me explain."

Angie then recalled the whole story to a dumbstruck Rusty. When she'd finished, she handed him the letter to read for himself. By the time he'd stopped asking questions, they were turning into the drive at Larchridge and he began to pay attention to his surroundings. "Wow Mom! Isn't this just something else?" was his much repeated response.

The Pringles were waiting to welcome them, with tea and scones ready on the kitchen table. While serving tea and chatting about the latest news on the estate, Mrs. Pringle couldn't take her eyes off Rusty. When Angie then introduced him as Mr. Anderson's son her face lit up with unmistakable pleasure. Eyes shining brightly she exclaimed, "I knew it was but I didn't like to be impertinent by asking. You're the image of your father, like two peas out of a pod. Wait till I tell my husband who you are. It'll make his day."

After doing the tour of the house, mother and son finally found themselves alone in Rob's studio where

174

Angie sat quietly gazing out of the window, while Rusty investigated his father's paintings. Eventually, she asked, "What do you think about it all? Are you angry with me? Are you mad because I messed things up and now you've missed the chance to know your father? I wouldn't blame you if you were."

Rusty thought carefully before slowly answering, "I can't deny that I would have liked to meet him, which seems a normal enough wish to me. However, it's a weird story, making me think that I've been blessed with pretty weird parents who don't do 'normal'. At the same time, it's quite a romantic story. You guys must have really loved each other to do the things you did.

As a kid, whenever I asked about Dad it always seemed to make you edgy, so I just learned to stop thinking about him. You're a great mom, in fact the best. I've never really felt the need for anyone else in our family. Life for me was about me and Mom; that's the way it was. I suppose Dad decided to stay out of our lives for what he thought were good reasons. I have to respect him for that but there's still a tiny piece of me that says it would have been good to know him." Angie was sniffing into a tissue.

Rusty continued. "I'm not mad at you Mom. It couldn't have been easy for you. I just feel a little bit sad. Now come on, just look at that wide open space waiting for us to explore. Let's go and walk in Dad's footsteps to discover what he must have loved about this place. I've already fallen in love with the atmosphere in the house. Let's see how it feels out there, roaming the hills. While we're walking I can tell you all about my exploits in Europe. You're never going to believe what happened to us in Spain ..."

Back in the car, heading south on the motorway, Rusty turned to Angie. "I guess we should be proud of Dad. He must have gone through some pretty bad times, but he stuck to his guns. He's definitely my hero." Angie patted him on the arm and smiled. "Without any doubt, he was a very special person."

End of Summer

Rusty's next stop on his whistle-stop trip to England, was Wollingford. Angie had booked rooms at the County Hotel and had arranged for Dennis to meet them there for dinner that evening; unfortunately, Sandra couldn't make it as she was tied up with a prior engagement. Just as Angie had expected, Dennis and Rusty got on like a house on fire. They laughed, they joked and both told ridiculously funny tales resulting in a hilarious evening.

Next day, bright and early, Angie took her son to Millbeck, to show him where she and his forebears had lived. The village was looking at its best, basking in the warm September sunshine with the berries bright on the hedgerows and autumn fruit hanging from the trees. On the hills hovering above, the seasonal colours tinged the summer green with shades of brown and orange. A few old friends and neighbours remembered Angie from the past and gave her a friendly greeting, and even those who'd never set eyes on her before wished them both "Good morning," as they passed by.

After a tour of the village, including Ted and Marjorie's grave, the pair headed towards the garage, where Dennis was waiting for them, eager to show them how the new improvements were progressing.

"So what do you think of Millbeck now that you've had a look round," Dennis asked Rusty.

"What's not to like?" he replied. "I feel comfortable here already and I wish I could stay a little longer but the guys are waiting for me in London and we have our flights booked for L.A. I sure would like to make another trip, focussing on the U.K. next time. Perhaps next year." He turned to his mother and asked, "What I can't understand is why you ever left this great place Mom. Why?"

"I guess I just needed to know what was out there, beyond the boundaries of my cosy little world. You're fortunate enough to be able to take a vacation touring abroad, exploring foreign countries, but that wasn't an option for people like me; we didn't have those choices in our lives. Although we weren't poor, neither were we rich enough to afford the luxury of wandering round the world to see far off places. I was happy growing up here but I always had the spirit of adventure and wanted to find out how the rest of the world lived. I knew I could get work in America so I grasped the opportunity with both hands. The rest is history."

"Yeah, I guess. How about you Dennis? Didn't you have the spirit of adventure? Did you ever leave Millbeck?"

"I did have the spirit of adventure and when we were children we roamed far and wide in those hills up there till we knew them like the back of our hands. Like your mother, I'd have liked to break out to explore further afield when I was a young man but I wasn't free to do that. My father died when I was still at school, leaving me, as the eldest child, to help Mother look after the family. Somehow, I missed my moment and here I am, still in the same place, looking after my ailing mother and running a business in partnership with your mom. Let me show you round."

Having inspected the building work, they were back in Reception discussing plans when Rusty looked out at the petrol forecourt. "I've seen several of those small vehicles around the place and they've got me puzzled. What does that logo along the side mean? Is it a person, is it a company or what? I don't understand."

Dennis and Angie followed the direction of his gaze and burst out laughing. "That's no person; it's a company that sells upmarket fries, run by a person I knew as a child," his mother explained. She screwed up her eyes to look more closely, making for the door, exclaiming, "I don't believe it."

Angie walked up to the tall, fair man filling his car at the petrol pump. "Good morning Godfrey," she said. "This is a surprise. Not only did I not expect to meet you here, but is that Nick I spy in your passenger seat? What a turn-up for the books!" Without pausing, she strode up to the shiny black car with the gold logo, to tap on the passenger window. The stout, balding man inside looked at her blankly for a brief moment, then recognition spread across his red-veined face. "Angie. Angie Caswell." He heaved himself out of the car. "The last I heard of you was that you were living abroad somewhere. What brings you back to this neck of the woods?"

"Business, actually," she replied pleasantly. "I've invested in a business in Millbeck and I'm here for discussions with my partner on the details of the grand opening next week."

Nick looked confused. "Here in Millbeck, or in Wollingford?"

"Here. We've bought this garage and have great plans for it." Nick's jaw dropped as he looked across at Godfrey, who, having replaced the petrol pump, was listening very keenly to the conversation. "So you're behind that Esther Smith Finance," blurted out Nick accusingly.

"Oh! That's not all," Angie continued, still with a pleasant, innocent look on her face. "I hear there are big plans afoot at the Hall. The last I heard was that you've closed the deal with the development company who intend to go ahead with their plans for a new theme park there during the winter months; Reuben Goldberg Investments isn't it? I happen to have a seat on their board of directors. Tremendously exciting! What will you do now Nick? Are you still living in France or will you stay in this area? I'm sure Godfrey here would be only too pleased to give you a job helping sell his Posh Frites. Bonne chance, mon ami." With that, she turned on her heel to return to the grinning Dennis and the quizzical

Rusty. "What was that all about Mom," he asked quickly before Godfrey arrived to pay for his petrol. "I know you were up to no good; I can always tell by that look on your face and your body language."

"It's a long story," said Dennis, "but one which has a very happy ending for your triumphal mother. She's like an elephant, your mother; she never forgets. She's had a long wait, but look at the state of her now." Doubled up with laughter, Angie was escaping through the back door to gloat in private.

. . . . . .

With Rusty on his way back to L.A. and another five days to wait before the official reopening of the garage, Angie felt at something of a loose end, especially as she was eager to see her home again and wanted to ensure that Rusty returned to university with everything he needed. She rang Reuben for a friendly chat, only to be told that he was on vacation, so then she tried ringing Sandra.

"Hi Sandra. It's my last few days in the U.K. and I wondered what you're up to today. Are you busy or have you got time for your old buddy?"

"I'm glad you rang Angie. I need someone to cheer me up. I've hardly seen Asha this summer and thought she would be home by now so that we could at least spend a few days together. Instead, it turns out she called off to see her father and decided to stay a few days longer with him because she's been helping him sort out the business. That now means she'll only pay a flying visit here next week to collect her stuff, then she's off to university."

"That's a shame. I know how you miss her. What about Prem? When's he coming home?"

"He's managed to squeeze another four weeks out of the university on compassionate grounds. Also, he's suggested I go out there so that we can be together again. I've refused, of course."

"Why 'of course'?" asked a surprised Angie. "It sounds exciting to me."

"You don't know the full story. When we were married Prem's family looked on me as the shameless hussy who had tempted their golden boy into an unsatisfactory marriage. In their opinion he should have allowed his mother to choose a Hindu wife for him. None of them came to our wedding and I was never invited to meet them. Prem kept in touch and when his mother became seriously ill he visited as a sign of respect. When she died, the others went into a tizzy and Prem dashed out on his white charger to save the family fortunes. If I go out now, I won't see much of Prem because he'll be working on the business, and I'll be left with hostile family members. I can't see any fun in that."

"I get your drift," said Angie pensively. "I'm feeling a bit lonely myself. I'll only be back a couple of days before Rusty leaves home again and the apartment will seem so empty without his clatter and chatter. Why don't you come to L.A. with me and we can keep each other company until you're ready to return home? I'll need to go to the office occasionally, but that won't stop us from having a ball together. The flight's on me; remember, I told you I'd had a bit of luck recently." Sandra soon cheered up at the prospect of time in L.A. with her lively friend.

Five days later the population of Millbeck, the local press and the village brass band all turned out in the autumn sunshine to watch Mrs. Skillington bravely struggle from her wheelchair to stand in front of the big red satin ribbon draped across the entrance to the garage, to accept a huge pair of scissors from Angie. With no further ado, she faced the crowd and trying valiantly to raise her voice, she declared, "I'm proud to be able to say that this business will now be called Skillington Stop. I declare it open." With that, she cut through the red ribbon and flopped, exhausted but happy, back into her wheelchair. "Where's that cup of tea you promised me Dennis?" The supportive crowd cheered and sang heartily as the band struck up an energetic rendition of, 'For he's a jolly good fellow'. It was an elated Dennis who, on one of the proudest days of his life, wheeled his mother into the premises in which he now had a genuine half share.

Two days after that, Angie and Sandra were landing in Los Angeles airport, also bathed in sunshine but in a totally different type of atmosphere.

Back in U.S.A.

Although Angie had enjoyed her trip to the U.K., she was glad to be back in her comfortable apartment, at home amongst her own possessions. Her time with Rusty was very brief but they did manage to discuss the impact Rob's will might make on their lives.

"What will you do about Larchridge, Mom? Will you keep it or sell it to invest the proceeds into something else?"

"I'm not sure, Rusty. It's given me food for thought and nudged me into pondering just what I want to do with my life. You aren't going to need me as much as when you were younger and, in addition, I don't find the agency so fulfilling as in the past. It was enormously satisfying getting it off the ground and watching it grow, but there aren't many of the old faces left any more. Most of them have moved on to do other things. I see them socially but it's not the same at the agency. The new staff are pleasant and efficient but somehow it feels much more impersonal now. I feel slightly remote from it and need something else to replace it."

"Are you tempted to return to England? You seemed very happy there when I visited."

"That's another thing. When I was in England I missed America, and now that I'm home, I miss England."

"I think you might need time to clear your head Mom. Why don't you take a break? Isn't there anything that you've always dreamed about doing but never had any free time because of all your responsibilities? Dad said you had to live for both of you. Try living it up a little and when you've had enough, that's the time to start thinking about your future. It's a great opportunity. There must be something."

"You are so very sensible Rusty Caswell. Sometimes I just wonder who the parent is around here. What would I do without you? I'll think about your advice."

Delaying any major decisions regarding her future appealed to Angie. She racked her brains to think what it was that she'd really like to do with the golden opportunity staring her in the face. She'd always wanted to visit Alaska in the springtime but that would mean waiting another six months. She thought long and hard before she went running into Rusty's room shouting, "Eureka. I've found it."

"I didn't know you'd lost anything."

"No, no. I've found the thing I've always wanted to do. Your father and I used to talk about it as a kind of fantasy. Now, I can make our fantasy come true."

"So, what is it?"

"I'm going to cross America on a Harley Davidson."

After Rusty had stopped laughing he said, "That's the mom I know and love. Dad would be proud of you. Do it Mom. I want to tell everyone how cool my mom is. Don't forget to let Reuben know; that will bring a bit of colour to his cheek and a twinkle to his eye. Will you do the trip on your own or would you join some group activity? Don't tell me the rest; you're going to join Hell's Angels."

"That would be too much even for me. No, she doesn't know it yet, but I'm going to persuade Sandra to come with me. We couldn't manage those big bikes but it is possible to hire bikes with riders for this type of venture. Oh! I'm so excited. I'll go and tell Sandra then I'll get down to making arrangements."

When Sandra heard the news, she wasn't quite as enthusiastic as Angie or Rusty. "I don't know where you get your ideas Angie. You never change. You've always been the same as long as I've known you but I have to say, this has to be the craziest so far. Why would I want to travel thousands of miles on the back of a motor bike, especially with a couple of blokes I've never met? I went on a boyfriend's motor bike once when I was in my teens and it was so uncomfortable, I vowed never again."

For Angie, this reaction was not altogether unexpected. She'd known she would have to use all her powers of persuasion. "This is not just any bike; it's a Harley Davidson. Have you ever seen one Sandra? The only thing they have in common with the bikes of yesteryear is that they both run on two wheels. These modern machines cost an absolute fortune and are definitely built with comfort in mind. Most people would give their right arm for a trip on a Harley. I'll show you one tomorrow. You can even sit on one. If you're still not interested in the trip, don't worry about it; one of my other friends will jump at the chance."

Next day, the two friends visited the Harley shop where Sandra was encouraged to sit on the back of one of the gleaming machines. "Comfortable as an old porch chair," said the handsome young salesman. "Now, if you're new to biking, may I show you some of our accessories? We've just had our latest range come in and, if you don't mind my saying, some of them would look mighty fine on you." Sandra loved trying on the leathers, the helmets, the goggles and lapped up the flattery from the hunky salesman. For Angie, it was mission accomplished.

Two weeks later, suited and packed, they waited nervously in Angie's apartment for the arrival of their drivers. "What if we don't like these people?" asked Sandra. "How do we know they're O.K.? We could be abducted and sold into the white slave market. Anything could happen."

"For heaven's sake calm down. You're winding yourself up when there's no need. These two guys come with the best of references. I know someone who knows someone and they have specifically recommended them.

There they are now. Come on Sandra, let's feel the wind in our faces and BURN SOME RUBBER!"

They introduced themselves to the two, big, burly bikers proudly standing beside their prized machines. Sandra looked a little apprehensive but relaxed when the two men, Roy and Gene, responded politely in a surprisingly gentle tone of voice, which was not at all what she'd expected. They carefully explained the routine, confirmed the route they'd all previously agreed, then they were off on their carefree, cross country adventure. First stop, Las Vegas.

After an exhilarating drive along the dusty highways, late afternoon found the group cruising The Strip, excitedly pointing to the famous places the girls had heard of but had only ever dreamt of seeing. Eventually, they pulled up in front of the Flamingo, one of the oldest casinos in Vegas where Angie and Sandra had booked a room. Roy and Gene were meeting friends and the plan was for them to go their separate ways, then meet up next morning to continue their journey together.

Sandra was more excited than Angie could remember ever seeing her before. She'd loved travelling on the Harley, she liked the two guys and she was ecstatic about all the glam and glitz of the city. She could hardly wait to get out amongst the action and quickly set about unpacking the outfit she'd brought precisely for this occasion. One hour later, showered and pampered, the friends were ready to hit the scene.

They took a quick turn around the 'hot slots' then headed for a cocktail bar, planning to explore the casino later in the evening. There was certainly no shortage of choice, and so after a short stroll they pushed open the smoky glass doors of the dimly-lit Smooooth Katz Club where they settled themselves on two tall bar stools. The sophisticated cocktail menu was a further cause of excitement for Sandra. "I've never had cocktails before," she told her friend confidentially. "How about you?"

"Yes, I've tried a few, but this menu is somethin' else. I'm going to take the easy way out by asking the barman what his choice would be for us. After taking the advice of a very helpful barman, the two had settled into happy chatter, while sipping a couple of Katz Coooolers, when they suddenly heard a loud voice behind them saying, "Can I buy you ladies a drink?" They swivelled round on their stools to find a smartly-dressed man in his fifties beaming at them with a look of enquiry on his face. Angie slowly, deliberately, looked him up and down, then asked in return, "Can't you see we're engaged in an intense debate on the trans-global merits of modern interactionary constitutionalism? Do you plan to contribute anything to the discussion other than a drink?"

The smile quickly disappeared as his mouth dropped open to emit a loud, "Huh?"

"In that case," she continued in an impatient tone, "hit the road Jack." Both women turned back to face the bar. When the man was out of earshot they started to crack up with laughter. "Does he think we're a couple of tarts?" asked Sandra, "and what's all this highbrow stuff about interactionary constitutionalism?" "The answer to the first is yes," replied her friend, "and as for the second, it's complete fabrication on my part. Uh! Oh! Don't look now but I think I spy another one approaching on the right flank. Your turn this time."

Within seconds a Southern drawl came from behind. "Hi, I'm Walter B. Harman, Junior; Wal to my friends." They did the familiar slow swivel. "Can I buy you sweet ladies a drink?" This time, it was Sandra who ran a critical eye over the speaker. "Friends? Do we know you?" she queried.

"No, but I'd sure like to get to know you. Do I detect an English accent? I could listen to that all night."

"Not to my English accent, you couldn't. Listen Wal, if you're looking for tarts, the restaurant's in that direction." She pointed to the dark recesses of the club. "Now is this clear enough? SLING YOUR HOOK." With that, she turned her back on the despondent Wal and resumed sipping her cocktail.

"Well done," laughed Angie. "Now, drink up. There's only one man I'm interested in tonight and I don't want to be late for his show. Sir Elton calls."

Despite a late night spent trying to explore as much of Vegas as possible in the limited time available, next morning saw the women up early, bright-eyed and bushy-tailed, ready to head off on the back of the bikes in the direction of the Hoover Dam and then on towards the Grand Canyon. The scenery was magnificent, the mode of transport exciting and by the end of the day a companionable relationship had been established between the four travellers. By late afternoon, having made good progress, they made a group decision to book in at a small attractive motel with a swimming pool and restaurant where they could all relax and cool down. After a few beers and a good dinner they were contented to turn in early, planning to head due east the next day on mainly minor roads with the intention of experiencing more of the natural beauty of the area.

The group spent a further two days blithely travelling through small towns and magnificent mountain scenery, until on the next morning Roy and Gene suggested they should make a slight detour by heading off towards a motel they knew in a small town up in the hills which was a popular stop for bikers. Angie and Sandra had no objections. They'd enjoyed their journey so far and would welcome the chance to meet others in the biking community.

After another day of magnificent scenery, stopping at small gas stations to buy food and drink to eat out in the open air, they arrived, early evening, at their destination. Rounding a bend in the steep road, the motel spread out before them in the old style of the late 1950s. The accommodation was laid out in neat rows, each with a parking space outside, around a reception office and a barbecue area. The guys had described it as quaint but on first impressions, the girls decided shabby summed it up more precisely. However, as long as the shower was in working order and the beds were clean, they were happy.

"Six-thirty at the barbecue," said Roy. "That's when the party kicks off. Are we going to have ourselves some fun tonight!" As the girls freshened up for the evening, they could hear the constant sound of bikes driving by to stop further along the row, then the cheery sound of friendly voices greeting newly arrived buddies. By the time they eventually stepped outside there was quite a buzz in the air and a general movement of party-goers in the direction of the barbecue area. Above the general hum, they heard someone calling their names and turned to see Roy and Gene beckoning them to join them on the blanket they'd laid out on the ground near a glowing camp fire. The mouth-watering smell of hot steak on the barbecue filled the early evening air and the convivial sound of guitars could be heard strumming country music in a far corner of the jovial crowd.

The group relaxed in the friendly, welcoming atmosphere, enjoying the juicy steaks and hot dogs, washed down by what turned out to be a constant supply of beer. Well-fed and watered, the crowd settled down in small groups around the camp fire to listen to the music, some quietly chatting amongst themselves and others joining in with the much-loved vocals. Lounging on the blanket, next to Sandra, Gene took out his tobacco tin and began to roll a cigarette. "Is that easy to do?" asked Sandra. "You do it so neatly. Why do you roll them when you can buy them?" Gene laughed. "Are you for real Sandra? You can't buy smokes like this from no shops. Try it." He handed it to her saying, "Take a good long drag and hold it before you exhale." When she'd stopped coughing and spluttering, she replied, "You're right Gene. That's nothing like the cigarettes I used to smoke." Nodding his head in agreement, Gene said, "That's some real top-class grass. Try some more." He passed it back to her. After taking another long drag Sandra returned it saying, "You are naughty Gene, getting me into bad habits. I've never smoked pot before."

"Ain't you never been to a party before?"

"Of course I've been to parties."

"Well what do you do at your parties if you don't smoke a joint or two?"

Sandra began to giggle. "I'll tell you what we do if you promise not to tell anyone." She leaned over and whispered in his ear, then they both burst out in uncontrollable laughter.

Angie, who was in conversation with Roy and another of his biker friends, looked round at the raucous pair beside her. "That sounds like a good one," she joked. "Can anyone join in?" At that, the two started to giggle even more. Angie rolled her eyes and turned back to where her two companions were still deep on conversation. As she did so, her attention was caught by raised voices across on the other side of the camp fire. Two women, one in tight blue denim jeans and a clingy black top, the other in a flowing, 'hippie', floral dress, were arguing loudly.

"I only asked him to dance with me."

"He's my man. Won't your own man dance with you or has he wandered again?"

"What do you mean? Wandered? Again?"

"I mean, leave my man alone and go sort out your own. I know you of old; I know what you're up to missy."

As their voices were getting louder and the tone more irate, an older man with snake tattoos up both arms, stepped in as peacemaker. "Come on girls," he said, "knock it off. Can't you see we're trying to party here? We guys didn't come all this way to listen to no cat fight.

Have another beer." He turned to a young guy throwing horse shoes with a group of friends. "Hey, Carlton, your sugar pie's gettin' lonely over here. Go get her a beer." Carlton walked towards the two women, put his arm around the one in the floral dress and walked off with her towards the beer table. The other woman went over to join in the banter with the group of men he'd just left.

While watching the fracas, although Angie had been vaguely aware of Sandra and Gene constantly giggling in the background, she'd ignored them, but now that the 'cat fight' was over she was disturbed to realize that the giggling had turned into a loud, slurred conversation and, what was that sickly odour hanging so heavily on the still, warm, evening air? Totally oblivious of anyone else around them, they had rolled off the blanket and were sitting on the grass with a friendly arm around each other's shoulders completely engrossed in their private conversation. Alarm bells rang for Angie.

Walking across to the couple, she took hold of Sandra's free hand to heave her to her feet. "Come on Sandra," she said. "Time for bed if we're to get away at a reasonable time tomorrow morning. I'm not sure what you two have been smoking but it sure as hell stinks. 'Night Gene." She slung one of Sandra's arms around her neck and supporting her friend as she stumbled along on wobbly legs, she asked, "Did you know what you were smoking Sandra?"

Sandra giggled, then burst into tears. Still slightly slurred, she wept, "Gene's my friend. He likes me and we were partying together. You have to smoke pot to party." Behind them, on the far side of the camp fire, Angie could hear the women's voices again. This time they were joined by the angry sound of men's raised voices.

Thankfully their room was not too far away. As soon as she lurched through the door Sandra made for the comfort of her bed. Still weeping she cried, "Why are you doing this Angie? I love Gene. He makes me feel good because he loves me. You're just jealous."

"Come on Sandra. You've had too much to drink and you're not used to smoking anything, let alone the dreaded weed. Lie back comfortably while I cover you up." Within seconds the recumbent Sandra was sleeping like a babe. Seizing the moment, Angie grabbed the room key and ran over to Reception to find Arnie, the manager of the site, to ask him a big, big favour. With her mission successfully accomplished, she then hurtled back to their room as fast as her legs could carry her.

Slipping quietly around the room, she grabbed their bags and packed their few possessions. Next, she placed a damp, cool cloth on Sandra's forehead and, with great difficulty, tried to rouse her. "On your feet," Angie ordered her bewildered friend. "We're out of here. Grab your bag and move. Now." Outside she bundled Sandra into the parked pick-up truck she'd just bought from Arnie, turned on the ignition and tore out of the motel car park like a bat out of hell. In the distance they could hear the sound of approaching police sirens.

"What's happening?" asked a befuddled Sandra. "Why are we in this strange car and where's Gene and Roy?" A procession of three police cars passed them driving in the opposite direction, lights flashing, sirens blaring. "What's happening Angie? Where's Gene? He's my friend." The tears began to flow again.

"We've had to leave him behind. Forget him."

Sandra wailed emotionally, "Turn around. I can't leave him. He loves me."

"No he doesn't love you. He's gay and he loves Roy."

"You're just saying that. Anyway, how would you know whether or not he's gay?"

"Because I arranged it that way. I told the tour company we were not looking for romance and they told me they knew just the right couple of riders for us. I forgot to tell them we weren't looking for the drug experience either." Sandra's sobs and tears had been replaced by a scowl, as she snuffled into a tissue. Angie continued with, "Anyway, you're married to Prem. What would he think about you fancying a biker? I thought he was the love of your life and yet here you are making a hullaballoo about a guy you've only known for a few days. Are you really that fickle Sandra?"

"You don't understand Angie. Why are you being so horrid to me? Why did you have to remind me of Prem when I'm missing him so badly. Of course I love Prem and I can't tell you how unbearably empty my life is when he's not with me. I wish he were here right this minute. I finally managed not to think about him this evening and now you've reminded me. When did you turn so cold and cruel Angie Caswell?" Black mascara runs were staining her flushed cheeks.

An increasingly irritable Angie exploded impatiently, "It's alright for you to call me names Sandra but I had to grow up quickly when I raised my son all on my own. You've always had a husband to lean on and a fat lot of good it's done you. You've grown self-centred instead of just growing up. That's what you really need to do; grow up!"

A shocked Sandra stared at her, open-mouthed, speechless.

"Now, if you don't mind," continued Angie grimly, "I've got to concentrate on driving this thing safely. Help me either by navigating or by shutting up and going to sleep. Just give me a break." Sandra chose the latter option, allowing Angie to concentrate on the road for the next couple of hours before they booked in to accommodation for the night.

Turning Point

By the time Sandra awoke, Angie had already been out to buy them coffee and doughnuts for breakfast. Sandra groaned as she lifted her head from the pillow, screwing up her eyes against the morning sunlight filling the simple room.

"What's the time," she croaked. "Ugh! My mouth is so dry and my head feels as though someone has used it as a football. I feel awful."

"Try some of this coffee," suggested Angie. "You're completely hungover and need some fluid to rehydrate you. Keep drinking anything except alcohol and we won't mention the smokes."

Sandra leaned back on the pillows, trying to sip the hot coffee. Looking puzzled, she commented, "I'm confused about last night. I remember smoking pot but why did that make it necessary for us to leave the place in such a hurry? Everything seemed to be going so well. I have this vague memory of being bundled into a truck with the sound of police sirens all around. What was it all about? Have I done something wrong? Are we on the run from the police and where are we?"

Angie shook her head. "No, of course we're not on the run but we had to get out of there before the police arrived. You were so out of it, you weren't aware of the tension building up around the two squabbling women over the other side of the fire. With all the drink and drugs swilling around, people were getting edgy and those women only had to light the blue touch paper for the whole place to erupt into violence. Arnie, of course, would have to call the police to sort it out and I didn't want to get caught up in that, especially with you in such a state.

Fortunately for you, I managed to get you back to the room then go and ask Arnie if he would sell me his pick-up truck so that we could get the hell out of there. He told me he was used to the situation and was poised to ring the police as soon as the fighting broke out. He agreed to sell me the truck and promised not to ring the police until after we'd left because he knew we were 'ladies' and he couldn't understand what we were doing with that low lot."

"They weren't low," Sandra interjected, "I liked them. They just kept some strange company."

"Yeah, they should've known better than to introduce us to them. Anyway, let's put it behind us. I've always fancied driving a pick-up but never had the opportunity. I've always envied people I've seen slinging their stuff into the back of the truck and casually driving off. I've sorted out a route, so let's do it just as soon as you get yourself together."

After a couple of hours spent driving along country roads with hardly another vehicle in sight, Sandra asked Angie, "Was I badly behaved last night? It's all a bit blurred but I have a nasty feeling I had an argument with you. Do I owe you an apology or something?"

"Honestly? Yes, you were badly behaved. You shouldn't have smoked pot and you should have known better than to try making up to Gene. It wasn't exactly your proudest moment. Also, you didn't make it easy for me when I was trying to do my best. In fact, you were downright rude and hurtful. I'd had more than enough of you last night. As for owing me an apology, that's up to you to decide; it doesn't change anything."

Sandra looked aghast at her friend. "I'm so ashamed Angie. I didn't realize I'd been so objectionable. After all you've done for me! I promise it won't ever happen again. Cross my heart."

"Bet your boots it won't happen again. You really pushed me to the edge this time. Anyway, that's history; let's not waste today. Where else would we see a view like this? I expect to see Clint Eastwood galloping over the ridge any minute now with a posse chasing after him."

Another twelve days and about two thousand miles later saw the friends on their way to New York City. As their vacation motto had been 'no regrets', they'd taken up every challenge and opportunity that presented itself to them along the way. They'd been horse riding, rock climbing, kayaking and by sticking to the more minor roads they'd managed to see just about everything small town America had to offer. They loved the country fairs with their colourful processions, and the country music in the hill country, but now they were heading towards the Big Apple where they'd part company as Sandra was flying back home from there, while Angie would take a flight to Los Angeles with the intention of flying out to England sometime in the near future.

Angie broke the silence that had settled on the car. "Well, so what are your general impressions? Was it what you expected?"

"I'm not sure what I expected. However, I do know, without a shadow of a doubt, that it was the most fabulous holiday anyone could ever have. The sad thing is, it's ending tomorrow. You're terrific company Angie; I can't say I'm looking forward to going back to an empty house."

"I know what you mean," nodded Angie. "It's a bit of an anti-climax after all the excitement of travelling, but at least you'll have Prem to keep you company. Is he back in the U.K. now?"

Sandra turned her big, anxious brown eyes on her friend. "I don't know. I've had difficulty in contacting him over the past few days. The last time I spoke to him, he was unsure of his return date." Her lips began to tremble. "Do you think he really will come back Angie?"

"Why wouldn't he come back? Has he told you he won't be returning?"

Shaking the shiny dark hair, Sandra replied gloomily. "No, he hasn't said so in so many words but I can't help worrying. Everyone always leaves me; Dad left me, Robert left me and a big part of me feels the same will happen with Prem. I do truly love him and miss him every single day. What will I do without him? Do you think he's found someone else out in India who's more compatible than I am?" Deep sobs of self-pity began to rack her entire body.

Trying to keep her eyes on the road ahead, Angie patted her friend's lap comfortingly. "Come on, Sandra," she said softly. "Don't judge Prem in that negative way. You've been together for a good many years and there's never been a hint of him wanting to stray. Quite the reverse, in fact, judging from what you've told me. As soon as we get to the hotel and you can get a reliable land line, telephone him for a good, honest chat and find out what's happening. Get to the bottom of the matter instead of worrying about something that hasn't happened yet and isn't even likely to happen. Now, dry your eyes and help me find my way to the hotel. We're nearly there and we must concentrate."

By midday they'd managed to locate their hotel, where Angie soon sprang into action. First, she rang a car dealer and struck a deal whereby he'd relieve her of her beloved pick-up truck. Next, she pushed the telephone into Sandra's slightly unwilling hand with the instructions, "Ring Prem. Now. Get it sorted once and for all." Wearing a resigned expression, Sandra obliged by trying to get hold of her husband at the family shop in India but without any success. After a long wait she heard a voice at the other end saying, "Hello, hello." Encouraged, Sandra asked, "Could I please talk to my husband, Prem?" There was a pause, then the other person replied in some unintelligible language. "Do you speak English, please?" asked Sandra. Again, there was a pause, a response in an unintelligible language and after another pause the phone line went dead. As a last resort she rang Prem's family home in the hope that someone there might speak English and be able to help. The number rang out but no one answered the call.

A forlorn Sandra slumped into a chair. "What else can I do?" she asked, shrugging her shoulders. "It's hopeless."

"Nothing's ever hopeless," retorted her friend. "Just because you're not getting a response at the moment doesn't mean you have to give up. Try again at regular intervals and you'll eventually get hold of someone who can help you. In the meantime, how about 'no regrets?' Do you still want to see the Empire State Building? If so, I suggest we grab a quick sandwich before you go off to do some sightseeing because I have an appointment to see my business associate, my good old friend Reuben."

Sandra slowly turned over the suggestion in her mind. "I might never get back .to New York and then I'll wish I'd done it. No regrets; I'm off to the Empire State Building and whatever else I can fit into the afternoon. I'll be back here at six o'clock, ready to have another go at contacting Prem."

Sandra and Reuben had decided to meet at a coffee shop a couple of blocks away from his office; his face lit up as she walked through the doorway. He stood up to give her a hug, saying, "Just look at you; aren't you a joy to behold?"

Reuben looked well; a little older, a little more silver but still with a twinkle in his eyes and that soothing air of calmness about him. "When did you get back? Did it go well? What have you done with your friend; I thought I might meet her."

"It was absolutely brilliant," beamed Angie. "We both enjoyed every minute of the holiday but, much as I love her, I need a little break from Sandra right now. She's got personal problems which she'll have to resolve herself. I've given her all the help I'm able and now she's wearing me down just when I need all my energy to make decisions about my own life."

"What decisions are those, if I may ask?"

"As you know, I'm at a turning point, Reuben, and it's time to make some firm decisions. Life has changed quite drastically for me in L.A. The past few months have proved that the agency can thrive under Lauren's care, in addition to which it's made me realize I no longer get any stimulation from it. You and I have discussed that before. Also, Rusty is flapping his wings, which is the way it should be but it leaves me in an empty apartment with a social life that has declined over the past few years as so many of my friends have moved away from the area and keep in touch mainly by telephone or Christmas cards. Time for a change. What d'you think?"

"I couldn't agree with you more. What changes are you planning?"

"I'm torn. I've loved living in America and when I'm away I miss it. However, after revisiting my roots and setting up the new businesses in England, I miss all that when I'm away from there. I feel so uncertain, which is unusual for me, so I've decided that I'm not going to rush in and make a rash decision that I might regret. I shall keep my apartment in Paloma Bianca which provides a home for both Rusty and me here in the U.S.A. whenever we want to use it. In addition, I shall set up a home in England. I shall enjoy being involved in our new businesses and I need to think about what to do with Larchridge. Should I make a home there or should I develop it into some sort of business? Perhaps both? At the moment, I feel such strong attachments to both of my properties, I'm unwilling to sell either of them."

Reuben gave her one of his slow, reassuring smiles. "I'm truly impressed Angie," he told her. "You're wise not to make any decisions you might regret. It sounds to me as though the balance is tipping in favour of England right now; that's currently where the action is for you. I'm going to miss you a whole lot. It's strange because although we keep in touch mainly by telephone, it's always been a great comfort to me, knowing you were here in America. Be sure to lift that phone at regular intervals, won't you?"

"I'll always be in touch, you can be sure of that. Anyway, Reuben, the world is a smaller place these days. How about you and Rebekah coming to visit me in England. I know you'd love it."

Reuben shook his wise old silver head. "It's kind of you to offer and I know Rebekah would love to visit but let me explain something to you, something that happened before you were even born. In those bad old days the Nazi regime in Germany scarred me, together with many more of my kind, for life; the terror they created haunts me to this day. It was with enormous difficulty that I managed to make arrangements for me, my wife, her mother and our baby daughter to escape the daily horrors by sailing to the U.S.A. but everything was hugely chaotic, making it impossible for the whole family to get berths on the same ship; we had to take what we could get. So, I boarded one ship and my family were to travel on another ship two days later. I didn't hear until after I arrived in this country that we'd acted too late; tragically, my wife, daughter and my mother-in-law had fallen into the hands of the Nazis, never to be seen again.

Ignorant of the fate of my family, when I initially landed here I rejoiced in an overwhelming sense of safety, followed by an ecstatic feeling of freedom I'd never before experienced. I was euphoric until I was made aware of the bitter truth, when my newfound joy quickly turned to inconsolable grief at the loss of my loved ones. Existing in a state of numbness, I thought I would never recover, but life has a way of continuing and I eventually emerged from my darkness, with that feeling of safety and freedom intact. That feeling has never left me and I give thanks for it every day of my life. Since setting foot on American soil, I have never left the shores of this country, even for a day. This is my home, I love it and here I'm safe and free to do as I wish within the laws. Rebekah has tried many times to persuade me to take a vacation abroad, to see something more of this world but I'm still not brave enough to leave my sanctuary. Whenever I come close to agreeing to please her, I panic. I'm overcome by a ruthless, debilitating anxiety."

Angie took hold of his hand. "I'll never mention it again Reuben. You've battled with horrendous demons from the past and I'm sorry if I've disturbed some of them. Stay safe in the freedom you've found here. If Rebekah ever gets itchy feet again, put her on to me and I'll diffuse the situation by inviting her over to visit me. I'd make sure we both had a good time without worrying you.

"Thanks Angie; we might take you up on that. Speaking of Rebekah, she's been asking about you and Rusty, wondering when she's going to see you both again. It's been a while."

"Give her my love and tell her I promise to drop by the next time I'm in the U.S. It's been wonderful to see you again, you mean so much to me. However, the afternoon has flown by and I must dash. I have a last evening to spend with Sandra before we go our separate ways tomorrow."

Back at the hotel, a considerably more cheerful Sandra was waiting for Angie. "I've been thinking about our conversation," she said, "and I've decided that instead of waiting for something to happen, I have to make it happen myself. You were right in saying I've become too dependent on others over the years. I'm going to ring Prem to find out exactly what his plans are. In fact, I shall ring him right now."

"Hang on a minute Sandra, I too have had thoughts. Have you worked out the time differences between New York and India? I had a look at it for you and worked out that when you rang the other day, it was probably late evening in India and you may have got through to the night security guy. If you ring now, it'll be in the middle of the night, which isn't the best time to have a conversation with anyone except an insomniac."

"Of course, how stupid of me," laughed Sandra. "That explains it. I'd got used to the time difference in the U.K., but I got confused through being in the U.S.A. and forgot to make allowances. I think I'll be best to leave it and get in touch with him when I'm back home. Let's get packing for that early start tomorrow."

Freedom

Back in her apartment in Paloma, Angie was busy packing for her U.K. flight next day, when the phone rang. "Hi Angie, it's Sandra. Are you busy or have you got time to talk? I've a lot to tell you."

"My flight's not until tomorrow so I'm free until then. What's the latest from U.K.?"

"Let me give you the sad news first." Angie's heart skipped a beat. "Mrs. Skillington died so bring your funeral gear because she's to be buried at St. Mary's, the day after tomorrow at three o'clock."

"I'll be there," said Angie. "She'll be sadly missed. How's Dennis taken it?"

"Who knows? You never can tell with him when he covers up all his feelings to put on his Mr. Cheerful face. You know what he's like, but I think he's probably hurting inside."

"Yes, he's a big teddy bear at heart and he was devoted to his mother."

"I have more news for you. When I heard about Mrs. Skillington, it got me thinking about Mum so I went over to see her. I was expecting the usual frosty reception but that didn't happen. She made me a cup of tea then we sat by the fire for a chat. We spoke about the funeral and one thing led to another. She asked about Dennis, Prem and Asha and then finally got round to me. I told her about our holiday in America and I also told her about Robert's death as she'd always had a soft spot for him.

I was rather surprised to find Mum in a strange, reflective mood; a mood I didn't really recognize. She told me she'd probably been too hard on me in the past and that during the endless hours she's spent on her own, she's had plenty of time to regret it. She said she'd always tried to be a good Catholic but if she had her time over again she might do some things differently. As a child, she was taught that if she was good she would go to heaven and the sinners would go down below. She actually said that although she'd done her best to do the right things, her life on earth, most times, had been a living hell as it had been so unbearably lonely. Do you remember her when she was younger, Angie? She was always so smart and attractive. Well, apparently she wasn't short of attention from the opposite sex but she turned them all away because she believed she was married to father for life, even though they were legally divorced. She went on to say that even though she has plenty of friends at the W.I. and the Knitting Circle, she still comes home to the silence of an empty house. As far as she's concerned, nothing can make up for not having someone close with whom to share your life.

As far as Prem was concerned, she said she was sorry her religious beliefs had influenced the way she treated him. Mum actually told me she should have trusted me to make my own choices instead of being so judgemental. After all, it was my life not hers. She went on to admit that, despite the circumstances, she's glad Prem and I are happy together and forever thankful that I haven't had to suffer the loneliness that she endures to this day. I could hardly believe my own ears when she said she'd like to get to know him and invited us to lunch on Sunday."

"Is Prem back in the U.K.?"

"Yes. I was saving my best piece of news till last. I arrived home intending to phone Prem in India, so you can imagine my absolute astonishment when I opened the door to find him standing in the hall, arms open wide to welcome me home. I'll never forget that indescribable moment. I don't ever want to be parted from him again and will follow him to the ends of the earth rather than be without him."

"So what are his plans? Can the family manage without him now?"

"Well, that's my next surprise. While he was out in India he carried out some initial research on a project he's had on his mind for quite some time. When he wrote it up and presented the paper to his department, they were favourably impressed and have agreed to him taking a year's sabbatical to give him the opportunity to continue with his study. He wants me to go back to India with him so that I can help run the family's sari and silk shop to free him up to do his research. I've learned my lesson and was there like a shot, discussing his ideas and making plans with him. The only fly in the ointment was Mum. I wasn't sure about leaving her for a whole year and that's partly why I went to see her. I hadn't reckoned on her new frame of mind and was relieved to find that she gave me her blessing and encouragement. She refused my invitation to come and visit us in India but said she'd look forward to regular reports on my adventure. She was genuinely pleased for me so it's next stop India for me with my darling Prem at my side. Isn't it exciting?"

"It's thrilling Sandra. You have to admire your mother; it's a huge step for her to take and I'm glad she's released you from that heavy burden of guilt you've been lugging around for so long."

"Thanks Angie. I'll see you at the funeral. Safe journey."

After an uneventful journey, Angie found herself once more in the old familiar surroundings of St. Mary's churchyard. The funeral had been well-attended by locals and family all intent on celebrating the long life of Mrs. Skillington. Angie waited until the last well-wisher had shaken hands with Dennis before going over to give him a big hug. His face lit up at the sight of her.

"How are you doing?" she enquired.

"I'm fine. Mother had a good innings and was becoming very frail."

"No, I mean how are you really doing? Are you really fine? Your mother was such a strong character; she must have left an enormous gaping hole in your life." She tucked her arm in his as they walked towards the church gate.

"Every word you say is true and I miss her more than I ever expected, even though she told me only the other day that she wouldn't be with us much longer. She thanked me for being a good son and hoped she hadn't been too much of a burden." Dennis paused to turn his face away while he cleared his throat. "She was certainly one of a kind." Angie squeezed his arm as they continued on their way to the Skillington cottage where Mandy had laid on tea and sandwiches, in the traditional way, for family and close friends.

By early evening the visitors had left, the house had been tidied and Mandy had gone back to her own home. Dennis and Angie were left sitting in front of the fire, the silence broken only by the occasional spark from the logs in the grate.

"What now then?" asked Angie. "This must be the first time since you were fifteen that you haven't had family responsibilities. Does it feel strange?"

"In truth, Angie, everything feels strange. My life and this house has always been so full of people who, one by one have left to go their own way. Every working day I've gone out to my job, knowing I have to work because others are depending on me. Without wishing ill on anyone, I looked forward to the day when I'd be relieved of that burden and would be able to do as I chose. Now that time has arrived, I don't know what to do with myself. I can't eat. I can't drink. Everything is topsy turvy. There's no meaning to anything anymore, except, perhaps, the garage. I think I'll probably go back to work there tomorrow; at least I'll be able to do something useful."

"Oh! That's a shame," she said, pulling a face. "I was hoping you'd do me a favour tomorrow. I need to take a trip up to Yorkshire but as I'm a bit jet-lagged I was wondering if you'd like to drive me. It's a beautiful run up there."

"Yorkshire? I'd intended to get back to work tomorrow. What's so important up in Yorkshire?"

"I have a house up there that I'd like you to see. I've inherited it and I'm not sure what to do with it. I'd like your opinion on it."

Dennis sat staring at her. "Are you having me on? Inherited? A house? How's that come about?"

"How long have you got? It's a very long story and I might need a glass of whisky from that bottle over there to get through it." Dennis brought out two glasses and the bottle of Scotch while Angie proceeded to tell him her tale.

Several hours and a bottle of whisky later, they were still discussing the details of Angie's past and its impact on her present circumstances. Dennis rumpled his unruly hair. "So you've told Sandra that he's dead but not about how you've inherited everything? Isn't that going to be awkward? I don't understand."

"Yes, it would be awkward if I didn't have plans to tell her everything. I've waited because she's had a lot of heavy problems to deal with just lately. I wasn't sure how she'd react when she was feeling so depressed but now that she's up and on top of things again, I'll bring her up to date. She'll be O.K. about it. Is there anything left in that bottle or have we finished it off?"

Dennis held up the bottle, shaking his head ruefully. "All gone but there's another where that came from, if you like?"

Angie shook her head. "I think I'd better be on my way. It's getting late." She tried to stand up, without much success. "I seem to have lost the use of my legs," she giggled, sinking back into the comfort of the old sofa. "Are you sure you drank your fair share, Skillington?"

"I've drunk more than I've drunk in ages," he replied. "You're a bad influence on me Angie Caswell." That made her giggle even more. "That settles it then," she told him, trying to keep a straight face. "You can't drive me back to Wollingford in that condition so I'll have to stay the night."

"What are you talking about? Who said I was driving you home?"

"Me, except I forgot to tell you. I came to Millbeck by taxi because I didn't arrive until after midday and came here straight from the station, left my luggage in safe-keeping at the garage, then went on to the church. I'll sort it all out tomorrow but now, if you don't mind, you're sitting on my bed and I don't think I can keep my eyes open much longer."

Next morning, Angie awoke, vaguely aware of a presence in the room. Slowly raising her reluctant eyelids, she squinted over the top of the warm woollen blanket that was covering her. In those first few seconds she didn't recognize her surroundings nor did she understand why she was sleeping on a sofa instead of a bed, then it all came rushing back. She sat up, peering over to where she could hear the sound of curtains rattling along the curtain poles as someone pulled them open. It was Mandy, bright and friendly, smiling at her as though there were nothing amiss.

"Morning Angie. Looks as though you and our Dennis were on a bit of a heavy one last night." She waved the empty bottle and picked up the two tell-tale glasses. What's it going to be, tea or coffee, unless, of course, you fancy a hair of the dog?"

Angie stood up, stretching and yawning. "My head feels terrible and my mouth feels even worse. Coffee would be fantastic, thanks Mandy."

"I see you're very privileged," continued Mandy. "Our Dennis doesn't lend his favourite tee shirt to just anybody. Very snazzy." She disappeared into the kitchen, leaving a puzzled Angie to look more carefully at what she was wearing. It turned out to be a huge red top with 'Weaver's Darts Team' stamped in large yellow lettering across the chest. "Privileged?"

There was the sound of heavy feet clattering down the stairs, then the door burst open to reveal the owner of the garment in question. "Morning Angie. Hi Mandy. What do you think of this one trying to ruin my reputation? Whatever will the neighbours think?"

"When did anybody in this family ever think about reputations or what the neighbours think," was the response from the kitchen. "Their lives would have been horribly boring over the years if it hadn't been for us Skillingtons."

"Don't blame me," chimed in Angie. "He's a very willing participant who's agreed to take me up to Yorkshire today for a weekend away." Dennis stopped still in his tracks. "Who said anything about a weekend? I thought I was driving you up and returning later today."

Angie smiled sweetly. "I probably didn't explain myself properly, being under the influence of your very generous hospitality. There's so much I want to show you up there and I think you'll love it. Don't forget to pack your walking boots." She gave Mandy a 'look' as she returned with two welcome mugs of coffee; Mandy got the message.

"Go on Dennis. When did you last take time off? There's nothing to keep you here. We've got staff in over the weekend and I'll be on call. I'll go and pack you a bag while you have your coffee."

Quickly realizing that his feeble protests were no match against the onslaught of their female persuasion, Dennis found himself, a couple of hours later, driving his car north with Angie in the passenger seat and his overnight bag plus walking boots packed away in the boot. As they turned off the motorway to drive through the small hamlets and open countryside, Angie could see his tired, strained face visibly relax. "This is starting to look like my kind of countryside," he told her. "Is it much further?"

"Next right."

His jaw dropped open as he finally entered the drive up to the house, to be confronted by the sight of the graceful larches, still wearing the remains of their fiery autumn colours, swaying gently as the car passed by. "You can't beat the larches for colour," he said admiringly. "They've always been one of my favourites. I see it's a private drive we're on; who's the owner?"

"I am."

Before he could reply, the house came into view. "I suppose you're going to tell me you own that too," he said flippantly. "It's very grand. Is your little house behind it?"

"No, that's my house. That's where we're going to stay. I also own a lot of land round and about, including part of the moor to the rear. Come on; I'm dying to show you."

The pair spent a happy couple of days exploring the area and decided to take one final walk before returning to Millbeck. Rambling through the fields and over the stone walls behind Larchridge, they soon left all traces of civilisation behind as they headed up onto the open moorland, ablaze with the golds and browns of late autumn. Sitting on a rock in the watery afternoon sunshine, they looked down on the world below.

Breaking the silence, Angie asked, "What do you think of the place? What are your first impressions?"

Turning to face her, he replied, "I think my first impressions will also be my lasting impressions. I love it. I certainly didn't expect it to be so huge, but I love everything about it. It's easy to understand why anybody would choose to spend time here."

"What is it about the place that really grabs you?"

He stared into the distance for a while before answering. "It liberates the soul."

"That's very profound, coming from you. What do you mean by it?"

"It's the only way I can describe what it does to me. When I sit up here in this endless space, where I can reach out to touch the clouds, I see the tiny houses with their little puffs of smoke from the chimneys, the miniature church and the occasional dot of colour where there's a vehicle. I know there are people down there struggling with their problems but all of it is non-existent when I'm up here. I'm at one with nature and it releases something inside me. What goes on down there," he explained, pointing towards the houses, "comes and goes but all this goes on forever. Compared with this, any problems I have are of no consequence; they disappear in the mists of time. That's why I say it liberates the soul. It's hard to explain. Can you understand what I'm trying to say?"

"I know exactly what you mean because I get the same sensation when I'm up here. I'm delighted that we share the same feelings about the place. That's why I want to ask you something important."

"Oh! You don't want to marry me, do you?"

"Are you asking or protesting?"

"Forget I said anything."

"What do you think I should do with this property? What would you do with it?"

"If it were mine, I certainly wouldn't want to sell it. I suppose it depends on whether you can afford to keep it because there are quite heavy overheads. You say you get income from the farming but there's maintenance of the property and the expense of keeping the Pringles as caretakers. Have you got enough to cope with it? What would you like to do with it?"

"I'd like to share it with you."

"How do you mean? Share it? It's yours."

"Yes, and eventually Rusty will inherit it because I really can't bear to sell it even though I'm aware that at some time in the future there may be heavy expenses here. I know I'm fortunate to be so comfortably off, but despite everything I own, I see a lonely future stretching ahead of me. I need someone to share my life, someone close. You're my best friend in the whole world and I feel happy when I'm with you." She paused as he was about to say something. "Don't you dare treat this as a joke Dennis Skillington. I don't want to marry you. I want you to feel you can choose to do whatever you like. Goodness knows, I don't want to be the one to tie you down to responsibilities when those you were landed with in your youth have only just come to an end. I want a life where we can both choose to be free to come and go at will but where we are close enough to share the small things in life as well as all the other things that happen."

"Let me get this quite clear, Angie. What precisely are you proposing? Would we live together? If so, where exactly would we live?"

"Anywhere and everywhere; we have several choices. I have my apartment in L.A., you have your house in Millbeck and I would like you to help me develop some kind of business here at Larchridge so that together we can continue to enjoy everything this wonderful place has to offer."

Dennis, looking very serious, was listening intently to every word she uttered. "I'll need time to think about this, Angie. How long have I got? Are you an easy person to live with? Are you tidy around the house? Do you slurp when you drink your tea? Do you ...?" A well-placed thump landed on his shoulder.

"You stop this Dennis Skillington. Do you want to give it a go, yes or no? If it doesn't work out, I promise to unlock the door and let you go so that you can continue on your merry way, free as a bird."

"The truth is, Angie, I love being with you and always have done. I can't think of anyone I'd rather live with, AND, as this is the best offer I've had today, let's give it a go."

Angie threw her arms around his neck and kissed him on the cheek. "Fantastic. You had me worried for a minute there. That was a rotten trick to play Skillington." With that, she sprang to her feet, pushed him off his perch on the rock, and ran off down through the heather, blonde hair streaming behind her, shouting, "Beat you to the stile at the bottom corner." She could hear his feet pounding behind her as they both ran, free as the wind, to collapse in a panting laughing heap at the bottom of the slope.

AUTHOR

Ever since her childhood in the North East of England, Val R. Brown has loved reading and writing both stories and poetry. Her early ambition was to be a writer but that had to be put on the back burner for several decades.

A grammar school girl and one of a large family, Val left school aged fifteen to complete a year's commercial course which enabled her to earn an income as a Private Secretary. Since that time she has trained and qualified as a Social Worker, run an antique shop in partnership with her husband, as well as working on a voluntary basis in a women's refuge and adult literacy centres. Eventually she decided it was time to return to that original childhood ambition.

In the meantime Val has also raised four children and remained happily married for many years to her much-loved husband, John. She moved to Warwickshire when she was in her teens and although she has lived there for the majority of her life, she has also enjoyed moving around, including spending an interesting year living in U.S.A. Val considers herself to be a Student of the World, believing academic study has its role but life experience is the greatest teacher of all.

OTHER BOOKS BY THIS AUTHOR

The Girl in the Velvet Slippers. Pub.2014

The Girl in the Velvet Slippers, first published in 2014 to coincide with the centenary of Olive's birth in 1914, not only chronicles her life but frames it within a social setting which saw gradual changes over the century.

This thought provoking book will be of huge appeal to anyone with an interest in social history or the women's movement in the U.K.

A Bit Of What You Fancy... Pub. 2014

In the mood for a short read? Enjoy a relaxing stroll through this random selection of short stories by Val R. Brown, a writer who is at her best when she is story telling.

The collection reflects Val's particular love of the short story, demonstrating throughout her irrepressible sense of humour as well as an ability to address a wide variety of situations and relationships.

A Little Bit More... Pub. 2015

Another entertaining book of short stories from Val R. Brown. As ever, her stories flow as she subtly introduces a wide variety of characters and topics, giving rich food for thought while at the same time leaving much to the imagination of the reader.

Also included, for the first time, are some of her poems written in her own inimitable style.

Made in the USA
Charleston, SC
06 January 2017